THE PRICE OF HONOR

HONOR TRILOGY: BOOK 3

LYRA THORSSON

CHAPTER I

Rebecca

I should have seen all this coming. But I hadn't, and now I was in a mess I didn't want to be a part of. Not only that, but I had dragged Mary down with me.

Biting my nail, I tried to think of a way I could get out of this without her dying in the process. If I could, I would do anything to take Bastien down—

including risking my life—but Mary didn't deserve to die. She was far too young.

I paced back and forth in my cell. After the whole fiasco with the trial, Bastien and his men had dragged Mary and me out to a space transport on the other side of Regenwelt, had us go up to the spaceport, and forced us on a rather large cargo ship that had cells at the ready. How the hell he had pulled that off was beyond me. I figured he would go into hiding either somewhere on the planet or get away on a small stealthy ship. Instead, he was practically screaming to the universe that he owned it all and no one could stop him.

And perhaps that was the truth. Perhaps no one could ever stop him.

But I definitely wanted to be where it all went down. I wanted to witness his death—watch as his ivory tower goes up in an enormous set of flames. I would give my life to see that—and perhaps I would have to. As long as everyone else made it out alive.

If they weren't a part of it all, of course. I knew there were a lot of innocent lives that had, unfortunately, crossed Bastien and now were more corrupt than a drug dealer selling to a minor. I was one of those people. I knew I could never atone for the sins I had committed. Bardon was lying to himself if he thought I was innocent. I had done unspeakable things, and I deserved a cell as much as the others did.

Or perhaps I deserved to die.

I kicked the metal trash can that was next to the locked door. It hit the cold, hard wall with a loud thud. No one had come in here for days. Although I preferred the silent treatment from Bastien rather than having to look at him or hear his voice, I didn't like not knowing what was going on with Mary. The only reason I knew how much time had gone by was that I got three meals a day, passed through a small hatch at the bottom of the door. And the meals were quite pleasant. I had expected Bastien to force me to eat something I didn't want, and thus far, that had not been the case.

But I still wanted to know what was going on, where we were headed, and what his plan was. Although Bastien never told his full plan to anyone; nevertheless, I wished I could hear something from him so I could try to put the pieces together. But all was silent.

He was waiting for me to break.

I couldn't allow him that satisfaction. I couldn't let him get to me. That was what he wished for, and I would never, ever give him what he wanted.

On top of not hearing from Bastien, I also hadn't had any visits from Walrum. I thought he would be sent to taunt me, but I had been mistaken. Perhaps they all figured I knew what they would try to do, and so they decided to throw me a curveball. Or perhaps I was overthinking it all.

Or maybe I needed to break out of here myself and find the answers.

Unfortunately, there was only one way out of here, and that was by crawling through the vents. It was obvious, or at least it was in this situation. There were cameras in here, and I knew someone was watching my every move. If I tried to escape, there would be armed men wherever I dropped out, or they could gas me out. Either way, it would leave me vulnerable, and I didn't want that.

Which meant there was only one way to stop this silent treatment.

I crossed my arms and glanced up at one camera. "Fine. I'm ready to talk."

To be honest, I expected the door to immediately open and Bastien to be standing right there, as if he knew that was the exact moment I would ask for him. But it didn't, and I simply peered around, wondering if he would eventually come or if I had completely embarrassed myself. I wished I had a punching bag—I could pretend the bag was him. At least I would get some of this frustration out of my system.

He kept me waiting for what felt like over an hour. I didn't have a clock and was going off instinct by that point. The door slid open as I was lying in bed, staring up at the ceiling, counting the different ways I could murder the bastard. I quickly stood up as I hated being in anything but a ready position.

"You requested to talk to me, *meine Liebchen*?" He smiled—a smile I was all too familiar with. His green eyes watched me with such delight that I wanted to throw up—preferably on him.

My lips tightened as I clenched my hands. "Where is Mary?"

He let out a laugh. "Really? You are concerned for some girl you hardly know? That's very unlike you."

I didn't say anything but waited for him to answer my question. I had to admit, he was right about that. I had closed my heart and feelings off from everyone—but not because I didn't care. I did it because I knew if I showed any feelings for anyone, he would do whatever he could to ruin them.

But at this point, I couldn't fake not caring about Mary when she was already in his hands. Not after what had happened to Alexandra.

She wasn't supposed to die—her being alive and well was my only redemption. Or so I thought.

Bastien sighed. "She's fine. I wasn't going to hurt her. I don't need you more pissed off than you already are. Besides, she's my leverage to make sure you behave. I have her in another cell, and she's getting the best treatment I can offer."

"Let me see her."

He laughed again. "Oh, *meine Liebchen*, are you really that distrusting of me? After all this time?"

I didn't answer that. Of course I didn't trust him. He had made my life a living hell.

"Fine. I'll let you see her. But after that, I want you to come and talk with me. We have a lot to discuss."

I didn't like the sound of that, but if it meant seeing Mary and letting her know she would be fine, I was willing to take it. "All right then. Take me to her."

Bastien didn't say another word but turned his back to me and led the way. He was testing me, just like he always had. I could easily grab a weapon off him and kill him right there—but I knew that if I did, whoever was guarding Mary would execute her right on the spot. So I couldn't take my vengeance out on him—at least not yet.

As we moved, I tried to memorize the layout of the ship. Most ships of this size were similar in design, but I took note of where men were coming and going from, peeked into rooms to see what they were being used for, and noted anything else. I had a feeling Bastien knew what I was doing, but he said nothing and didn't try to take me in a direction that would confuse me.

After getting a feel for everything that was going on, I examined Bastien. He kept his hand behind him, as if he was pleased with his progress. His graying brown hair was even lighter than when I had left him. I hadn't taken the time to notice. If I didn't dye mine, I would find quite a few grays, mainly because of what he had put me through.

It was strange that even though I had the therapy for morphine, I didn't have that craving that typically came when I thought about facing Bastien. Perhaps because I was no longer full of fear but now was having to face my consequences. Fear was before a task, not necessarily during.

But I would be lying if I said my heart wasn't racing.

What if he wasn't taking me to her? What if he was lying and he was taking me somewhere to torture me? Did I care at this point? I was on a ship with dozens of men, in the middle of only Gott knew where. I doubted even Nik could get me out of this.

My heart hurt a little as I thought of him. I had been lying to him all this time, and my secret had come out in one of the worst ways imaginable. He acted like Bardon and assumed it wasn't my fault, but I could have stopped him. I could have said something a long time ago. I was neck deep in this, and my hands were as tainted as Bastien's at this point.

Yet he would still love me after everything, and that made it all the worse. I didn't deserve him, and he deserved someone better than me.

We halted in front of a door, and Bastien scanned his key card. The door slid opened, and I found Mary sitting on her bed. Her eyes were wide as she saw figures in the doorway. She drew her arms and legs in, still afraid of what might happen to her.

I glanced over at Bastien, who nodded. I rushed to her side and knelt down.

"It will be all right, you hear me? I'll make sure you are fine. Have they done anything to you?"

She shook her head. Her eyes were red from

crying. "No, no one has come in yet. You were the first."

So they did the same to her as they did to me. Although the silent treatment was scary, it was better than many alternatives.

"Good. I'll keep it that way. Don't worry, okay? I'll kill anyone who hurts you. And everyone here knows that, so you've nothing to fear. You'll be back to your brother and Samuel soon enough."

She nodded but said nothing. I let out a deep breath as I stood up and went to Bastien. The door slid shut and locked once again.

I turned to him and crossed my arms. "Well then, what did you want to discuss with me, Admiral?"

CHAPTER II

Nik

I had to find her—no matter what.

My leg shook as Bardon went through the plan. The plan was ever changing as we discovered more information on Sebastien's whereabouts—and by discovering I meant narrowing. We still had no idea where he could have gone to or where he believed he would find safety.

He had to have planned this out for a long time.

Sebastien knew we were after him—it was why he kept us on his team. That was how the saying went, I supposed: keep your friends close and your enemies even closer. With us around him, he would know our whereabouts and wouldn't have to worry. We should have noticed.

There was just the fact that no other human in existence would have been able to cover their tracks so thoroughly. How he managed it, I had no idea. He should have slipped up before this, but instead, it had gone on for years. I felt bad for all the lives that had been lost or corrupted because of him. We had tried our hardest, however, and after this trial, it was apparent that he had his hooks in many more men than we could have possibly realized. And they were still willing to protect him.

"Nik, *mon ami,* you still with us?" Bardon snapped me back to attention.

I blinked. "*Ja,* sorry. I'm just…"

"Worried about Rebecca. I know." Bardon let out a sigh as he looked at the screen. On the screen was a map of the systems with all the possible routes

Sebastien could have gone. We at least knew he left the planet, but that was as far as we had gotten. He could literally have traveled anywhere.

Jonathan nodded to the borders. "Do you think he'll be able to pass into another nation?"

Bardon shook his head. "He shouldn't be able to —his photo and name are on every roster, and aiding in his escape is a lifetime in prison. I would hope no one would let him through and that they will alert us."

"And yet so many helped him escape here."

Bardon frowned. "You're right. I didn't think they would. I knew Rebecca couldn't do anything about her part in it, and she did her best to try to help, but I never would have guessed that so many men would side with him."

"We were able to mitigate the number of deaths at least," Jonathan added.

I nodded. We did, but Alexandra still lost her life. I felt horrible that her life had been cut short. She did everything she could for this mission, and it still wasn't enough. I should have been able to save her—we should have clued her in more. But it was too late for all that.

And now Sebastien was out there, free as a bird. What's worse—he has Rebecca and is using Mary as leverage against her. I had a feeling Rebecca would do anything to keep her safe, and I didn't want to think what he would make her do.

"I still can't believe Sebastien was able to get Walrum to act how he did. A lot of the information he knew while we talked wasn't something I thought Sebastien knew." I sighed.

"It's likely he made Rebecca fill in the gaps." Bardon slid his finger on the screen. "I also put out a wanted poster, for her alive of course, in hopes of bringing her back."

"And then what? What will happen to Rebecca?"

Jonathan and Bardon exchanged glances. I hated it when they did that. Bardon was the one to answer. "She… will have to pay for her crimes."

I clenched my fist. "You said she would be free —you said her crimes would be wiped clean."

"And if she came forward with the truth instead of hiding it, then perhaps I could have gotten the other generals to look no further into it. But since

Sebastien was the one who confessed what she did and she was in on helping him escape, I'm not sure if I can get her off on parole or even a shorter sentence."

Great—that's all I needed to hear. That meant she had no reason to come back—no reason to turn Sebastien in. No, that was wrong. She wanted to see him burn more than all of them combined. But she didn't deserve to go to jail for that.

I bit at the dead skin on my lip. That didn't mean I couldn't do something about it—that didn't mean we couldn't go on the run again and find somewhere to hide. We had done it before, and we could easily do it again. First thing was first, however. I had to find her and Sebastien.

I glanced up at the map of the systems. If I were a sociopathic murderer, where would I hide? Well, if I knew him, he would go somewhere he was welcome and would do it while giving everyone else the middle finger. He had to be heading somewhere that he trusted or at least somewhere he knew he could control. Although there were clearly many people in the Nreff Nation that were helping him, whether because they supported him or were afraid of him, but he needed somewhere he knew no one would come after him.

He was going to go across the borders—I just knew it.

"Which nation was he tied closer to?" I asked as I stood up and glanced over the map somewhere. "He seemed to have ties no matter where he went."

"Oui, he did—or still does," Bardon commented. "But if I had to wager a guess, he had stronger ties with the YamaXie system than the Regit Republic. Or at least it seemed the YamaXie liked him more."

"Then I think we should send most of our men there in search of them. And to alert all the border patrol and make sure to station men we can trust at each checkpoint."

Jonathan let out an ironic laugh. "Like that will help. At this point, I'm not sure we can trust anyone other than the three of us in this room."

"So it's us against the entire universe. That sounds like fun."

Bardon frowned. "Unfortunately that is the case. There are a lot of people I don't trust. Sebastien did a good job, making everyone afraid of him. Although I didn't believe he would have been able to get everyone on his side, I'm not sure who to believe. We can send men out, but just because they report back that everything is clear, I don't think I can believe them."

He had a point there. I couldn't blame anyone for letting him get away with what he did—he had a way of persuading everyone to do his bidding. Any who stood up to him quickly disappeared.

"All right," I began. "Then I guess we are the ones who need to travel to YamaXie."

Bardon nodded. "I'll need to stay here just in case anything comes in about him or if I can see how he is pulling strings inside the military. The two of you can head out to the border and investigate whether he passed through. It's going to be a lot of paperwork and going through files, so to speak, but I think it may be the only way to figure out which direction they went after crossing the border. Even if knowing they are there narrows it down, there are still quite a few planets they could be on."

That was very true. It was strange to think of how vast the habitable universe was. I couldn't imagine what it was like in the olden days where everyone lived on Earth. It seemed like it would be very small even though there were still many places on Regenwelt I hadn't visited.

Which was why it was much harder to find Sebastien. We had camera systems that used facial recognition, but there were ways to get around those—Rebecca and I would know. There was also the problem of different systems not really caring who was on the wanted list in other nations. There were so many people out there they could barely keep track of their own people. Then there was the fact no one wanted to try to stop Sebastien.

I let out a sigh as I sat back down. This mission had been lasting for over two decades now, and it didn't feel as if we were any closer.

"What about Walrum?" I asked. "What are we going to do about him?"

Jonathan let out a deep breath as Bardon rubbed his eyes. It seemed Bardon had already been giving Walrum a lot of thought. "We are going to have to arrest him. He isn't the Walrum that we all knew. I doubt whatever Sebastien did to him can be undone. Whoever he is now is not the innocent man we once knew."

My heart felt as if it had sunk. Was Walrum really gone? Although for the longest time we thought he was dead, it still hurt. I thought we had a chance of having him back, and yet that was taken away from us.

But that meant I had a chance with Rebecca.

I hated myself for thinking that. I shouldn't have been thinking how this affected my relationship with her and focused on saving her—saving both of them. I wasn't going to give up on him just yet.

But we didn't have Alexandra. I felt horrible that she met her death when Sebastien shot her. She had done everything in her life to get back at him for killing her parents, but he ended up being her death as well. I wanted more than anything to go back and save her, but I couldn't. I felt as if I had messed up, and there was no way I could repent. I couldn't imagine what Rebecca was feeling right now and how she was dealing with Mary being in

Sebastien's grasp.

We would have to be careful—we would have to make sure she didn't get caught in the middle.

"All right then, which checkpoint should Jonathan and I head to first?"

CHAPTER III

Rebecca

I expected him to take me somewhere to torture me. Instead, he took me to a plain old conference room. As I stepped inside, I glanced around, expecting some catch—like a soldier ready to stab me or something. He gestured to the chair.

"Take a seat."

Sitting down, I watched as he pulled out the chair

across from me. He smiled like he always smiled—with a hint of sadistic delight on his face. I wanted to slap it out of him.

As he sat, he crossed his legs and gripped his knee as if he were thrilled I was across from him. He was silent for a moment, and I didn't particularly want to start the conversation.

"Well, *meine Puppen*, have you learned your lesson yet?" he asked.

My lip twitched. "My lesson? Remind me, which one is that exactly?"

He laughed. "Oh Rebecca, you like to say things you know will piss me off."

"Then I guess I haven't learned my lesson."

Bastien slammed his fist on the table, making me jump. "I am talking about siding with anyone other than me!"

My lips twitched. I was silent for a moment, but I knew I wasn't going to get out of this without answering his question. "You can't be serious, Bastien. You think after all the things you did—all the lies and deception and pure torture, that I would side with you willingly?"

Bastien frowned. "Do I think the person whom I love with all my heart would want to be at my side? *Ja, ich will.*"

I shook my head. "There is no way you actually believe that, is there? You don't love me. You just think you own me. I didn't think you had the capability of love in that cold, dark heart of yours. Stop lying to me."

I knew it was dangerous to say such things to him, but I didn't care anymore. He could hurt me all he wanted—I wasn't giving him the satisfaction of confessing I had any feelings left, because they were gone. I saw the demon that he was, and I would do whatever I could to take him down and keep Mary safe.

The anger disappeared from Bastien's face in an instant—as if it were a switch he could turn on and off, and if I hadn't known better, I believed he could. "Oh, dear Rebecca, you don't really believe that. Because if you did, you would know what pain it would bring you. I have kept your friend safe all this time, but if you decide that I'm not worthy of you, perhaps I don't need to keep her around any longer."

That right there was an example of not understanding love, not to mention he needed collateral to force me to stick around. I took in a deep breath and let it out.

"What's your plan? I can't imagine you can do anything except hide at this rate."

He laughed. "Do you really think I would hide after I have accomplished so much? *Nein*, I still have friends in other nations that can help me finish what I started?"

"Finish what? I never quite understood what your endgame was, Bastien. I always figured you simply liked torturing people."

"No, it's much more than that. I want there to be a war."

I turned and let out a laugh. "*Ein Krieg*? What would you gain in a war?"

His lips curled. "I have a large amount of stock in each and every manufacturing company for the armies. If a war started, I would be rich. We could go anywhere we wanted. We could rule—no one would question us."

"I think a lot of people would question us. Or you, really. I'd rather die than go ahead with that plan."

He slammed his fist on the table again and growled. "Why are you so difficult?"

I shrugged. "It's just who I am. It's why. You had such an interest in me—you thought you could break me of it. Clearly you were wrong."

Bastien stood up and walked to the other side of the table where I sat. I didn't let him see me shaking in fear of what he might do to me. I peered up at him and grimaced as his hand smacked me right in the face.

"I have shaped you! I have molded you into what you are today!" he shouted down at me. "You wouldn't be where you are if it hadn't been for me! You would have been stuck on the streets, wallowing in misery! No other general would take a cocky *Miststück* like yourself. I did you a favor!"

I knew he was lying—I knew Admiral Bardon would have hired me on, but I couldn't help but feel he was right. I had gotten as far as I did because of Bardon and then Bastien. Granted,

Bastien fucked me up, but where would I have been without him? Would any other general have hired me other than Bardon? And with Bardon it never felt as if it was because of my merit but because he felt sorry for me.

"I would have…," I began but didn't know what to say.

"You would have gone with Admiral Bardon? I know your connection with him, *Puppen*. I know your parents abused you and he was the principal of the academy at the time. He took pity on you, that is all. You never should have been allowed in."

I had been beaten, tortured, called names, threatened, and so on. This shouldn't have bothered me—I knew he was twisting the truth and that I was better than he was giving me credit for. I had aced all my tests, outperformed the men in my class, and was given high rankings at graduation.

But did any of the other admirals want me? Was I too much of a problem child for them?

I shook my head. "You are lying. I know you are. There is no way they wouldn't have taken me on. I was the best."

He lifted his hand, making me flinch. Instead of hitting me again, he stroked the side of my cheek. "You are only the best because I made you that way. If it weren't for me, you would still be that scared little girl trying to act tough."

I was going to make a sarcastic comeback but decided not to. All I needed was him yelling at me some more. So instead, I stayed quiet. He would take that as defeat—that much I knew.

But I was far from being defeated.

He was a *Schwein*—a jackass that needed to be destroyed. He made up lies—lies that crept under the skin and into someone's mind. If one wasn't too careful, they would start to believe them and would do whatever he said. He'd done it to me more than once. I had believed him when he said the people we'd tortured—the people we'd brought in to be experimented on—deserved it, that the nation wanted us to do it. I had believed he loved me once upon a time, but now I knew I was just his object— something that he simply didn't want anyone else to have.

And I would escape and be the one to bring him

down. Only then would I get my revenge—only then would he realize how mistaken he was. I was no one's little doll.

He brushed his finger across my lips, and I held back the urge to throw up. I just needed to get onto a planet; then this would be much, much easier. I would be able to rescue Mary and get her far away from this sadistic monster. Then I could come back and finish the job and not have to worry about anyone's safety. Not even my own.

Because I didn't care what happened to me as long as this man was dead.

Nik would care, and I knew that. I would have to finish this all before he found us, otherwise Bastien would be able to use him against me. Nik was the reason I went along with his plan on Regenwelt. If I didn't have Nik, I would have told Bardon everything. I still ended up making it a little better, but it cost Alexandra her life. She shouldn't have had to die—she was supposed to live. She was the only thing I did right in my life. Now, because of me and my stupidity, she was dead.

And this monster was alive and free.

I did need a backup plan, however, so I would have to leave clues for Nik and Bardon to be able to find us. I would just have to time it all right so they didn't show up before I ended it once and for all. It would be like a game—the sort of game Bastien always made me play with the law enforcement in the Nreff Nation.

Until then, I would have to convince him I wouldn't betray him. That wasn't going to be easy, not to mention I didn't want to. I wanted to be kicking and screaming until the end. I wanted to deal as much pain as I could every last second until his dying breath.

I took a moment to calm myself down. If I kept thinking about how much I wanted his death, I wouldn't be able to make this convincing. No, I need to have a level head and not fill my vision with red. This was only going to work if I had a clear mind and didn't think of all the hatred that filled my heart.

"Now, come. You are probably hungry. I prepared a meal for us in my private dining room. I was even kind and had them make something without meat for you."

He had prepared a meal for me? Did he know I was going to signal him today? I had a feeling in my gut that none of this was going to end well—for him or for me.

CHAPTER IV

Nik

Sebastien had people everywhere. He had contacts in every crevice of every dark alleyway. Why we kept going after him was beyond me. It seemed impossible to take him down. The only reason we thought we had succeeded was because he had let us catch him. He wanted it all to happen so he could begin his war.

So now he was fleeing to whatever nation he could to convince them to attack one another.

Why he wanted to do it was beyond me. To cause chaos? To wreak havoc? Because he was a monster in human form? Those were all plausible reasons. Part of me wanted to let it all happen and go hide in some wilderness somewhere. But I couldn't—I had to save Rebecca from his clutches.

Which was why we were headed to one of the border checkpoints—looking for Rebecca and making sure she was fine.

Well, that was why I was going to the border. Jonathan's mission was to stop Sebastien, but at that point I didn't really care. I wanted to save Rebecca and Mary from him. I didn't believe we could capture him. He had everyone wrapped around his little finger.

Jonathan and I were in a small space cruiser that could easily be manned by two people. I was glad we weren't traveling with anyone else as I didn't want to deal with anyone hearing what Jonathan and I discussed. Granted, we didn't have anything planned, but I had a feeling some matters would show their ugly heads sooner or later.

Such as what to do about Rebecca once we saved her.

Bardon said she would have to serve her time since she helped Sebastien more than once on missions. She confessed to it all, mainly due to Admiral Dr. Jørgensen's interference. He did get Sebastien to confess, however, but not without taking Rebecca down with him. Sebastien only did that because he was mad Rebecca had spent the night with him not once but multiple times. And while I felt a bit frustrated as well, he was on a whole different level.

Because Sebastien felt as if he owned her.

I clenched my fist. No one owned her. She was free to make her own choices. Even though, truthfully, those choices hurt. I understood she was hurting—I understood that she just needed to feel something and that what we had was complicated, but I wished she had come to me—I wished she'd told me the truth about everything before it was too late.

But then there was Walrum, and if she blew his

cover, Sebastien would have had me killed.

I let out a breath as I peered out the space shield at the stars. I missed our journeys together and wished we could have gone back to simpler times, although they were probably more complicated than I realized. Rebecca had always been peering over her back, and now I knew why.

Because Sebastien was always looking for her.

And because she had to get her morphine-B. I still wasn't sure how she was able to do that without me noticing something was up. She was in charge of the finances, however, so that was how she was able to pay for it. However, I still should have detected the side effects and her dosing herself. I felt like a complete idiot.

"*Est-ce que ça va?*" Jonathan asked as he glanced over at me from his seat.

I let out another breath. "Honestly, no. I'm stressing about Rebecca."

Jonathan paused for a moment, as if finding the right words. "That she is with Sebastien or about what Jacques said?"

"Both."

"She has committed crimes, Nik. And the higher-ups know about it now. She can't be just set free."

"I know, I know. I just… You saw her face when she was with him. He twists the truth and plays mental games. She probably had no choice. That should count for something."

"And it will definitely lower her sentence, but she wouldn't be free for a while."

After all this time, I couldn't let that happen. I shook my head. "That isn't fair."

"*Non*, what isn't fair is that a bunch of people helped Sebastien escape, and now we have to search for him because we are the only two Jacques can trust."

I frowned. "You think you are getting the worse end of this deal?"

"I didn't say that. I'm just frustrated that we have to redo this entire mission. We had been working on it for years, Nik. Then Rebecca went and messed it all up, just like she always does."

I stood. "She didn't mess it up, Jonathan. She was literally forced to do his bidding, otherwise he would have had us killed."

"I'm not mad at her—I'm mad at everyone else who helped him out. But even if her hands were tied for his escape, of which she did try to help us, I can't forgive her for never coming forward earlier."

I wanted to argue, but he had a point. Rebecca had enough evidence on him for almost the entire time she served him, but she never came forward. They had been on the mission for years and weren't able to find anything. Sebastien had known the truth—that the three of them were spies for Bardon, and he also knew that Rebecca wasn't one. How he was able to find out, I had no idea.

Not only that, however, he had brainwashed Rebecca into doing horrible things—making her think they were legal and for the good of the nation. I knew she hadn't realized until later what he had done to her and how, if she came forward, she would have had to confess all the things she did. It was clear she let guilt ruin her life—let it come between the two of them. She didn't think she deserved happiness. She didn't think she should be able to live out the rest of her life in happiness.

Which was why he needed to find her—before

she did anything stupid.

Well, not stupid. Just dangerous. I knew she would take it into her own hands to try to kill him. However, I doubted she cared about her well-being in the process. I wanted Sebastien to die a slow painful death as well but not at the risk of her life.

But at least I knew she wouldn't do anything until Mary was safe.

"How much longer until we reach the border?"

"At least another twenty-four hours."

"Great." It was going to be a long ride. Although space travel could be fun most of the time, it was not great when you were impatient. That went with any sort of travel, however. I hated sitting still, but at least on a ship there was some room to move around.

"Don't worry, we are going as fast as them. They only have had a day or two head start. We shouldn't be too far behind them."

"As long as we go to the right checkpoint—or if we are even correct on where he went to hide."

"Fair enough. Let's just pray that we chose the right one."

I sat down and leaned back in the chair. I didn't have much faith in any god after all the things I'd witnessed. If there were a god, I believed he or she was doing a lousy job running the universe. But I prayed to whatever thing was out there, whether it be fate, the universe, or a being, that we were heading in the correct direction and that we would be able to save Rebecca.

And then the two of us would run and hide for the rest of our days.

As we cruised forward, I heard a large crash come from the engine room. Both Jonathan and I were up in a flash—our guns at the ready.

Jonathan nodded for me to take the lead and that he was going to cover me. I slowly made my way to the engine room. I gestured to Jonathan to take the other side of the door. He jumped over, and we pushed the button to make the door slide open.

I wasn't sure what I expected had made the noise, but it wasn't what I found. It was Russ and Samuel. I put my gun away.

"Are you two *Dummköpfe*? What are you doing here?"

Russ folded his arms in front of himself. "Did you think I wouldn't tag along on a mission to save my *sorella*?"

"And my girlfriend," Samuel added.

Russ sighed. "This one followed me. I still haven't accepted him as my potential brother-in-law."

Samuel turned to him. "And how many times have I told you to stop calling me that?"

Russ shrugged. "Not sure what else to call you."

"Your sister's boyfriend. Or just Samuel."

Jonathan rubbed his temples. "I take it Jacques doesn't know you're here."

"Are you kidding?" Samuel laughed. "He wouldn't have authorized this."

"That's what I thought. Ugh, he's probably looking for you two and going insane."

Russ nodded. "Probably. But he should have figured we'd pull a stunt like this. I mean, we've always been in everyone's hair from day one."

Samuel nodded at Russ's comment. I laughed a little. It was like looking in a mirror. I put my hand on Jonathan's shoulder.

"It's good to see Bardon knows how to pick men and women with personalities. I think they'll be helpful. And would you let anyone stop you if someone kidnapped Bardon?"

Jonathan shook his head. "No, I wouldn't. I suppose they can stay, but you both realize this is dangerous, right? And that there is a high likelihood you'll be shot."

Both of them frowned and nodded.

"Anything for my *sorella*."

I let out a breath. "Rebecca will keep her safe. I know she will."

"No offense, Nik," Samuel began. "But I can't take your word on that. Not with everything she has done."

That was fair. Rebecca had done a lot of horrible things. But that guilt hung over her, and I doubted she would let another innocent person die. I saw that in her eyes.

But they didn't know her like I did. Everything they knew would make them not trust her. If I were in their shoes, I would have been worried about Mary as well. And while I knew Rebecca would do everything she could, even I doubted if that would be enough.

I turned toward the cockpit. "We better report to Bardon before he pops a blood vessel. He needs to know where you are."

"Fine," Russ whined. "But we aren't leaving the mission."

"Of course not," I commented. Because none of us would rest until this was finally over with. And I had a feeling it would be the mission of a lifetime.

CHAPTER V

Rebecca

I sat on my cot, staring at the gray walls.

Dinner went how I figured. It was quiet, awkward, and I wished I could go back to my room and eat by myself. I did my best not to make any comments to piss him off. But it went as well as it could, and I was back in my cell, waiting for whatever he had planned next.

We would have to hit a border sooner or later. He was making his way to the YamaXie territory, which I knew Bardon would deduce. At least that is what I hoped. Bardon was smart as he had been watching Bastien for all this time.

Except it took him this long to barely get any evidence against him. In fact, it was Rolf who was able to get him to confess since Bardon didn't have any solid evidence. Then he took me down with him.

I wasn't sure if I was mad at Rolf for what he did or not. I felt betrayed, embarrassed, and a little ashamed. I didn't think it mattered whether it was a man or a woman who slept around, as that was never anyone's business, but I saw Nik's face. We weren't ever officially together, and there was the whole Walrum thing, so it shouldn't have bothered me. But it did; it bothered me a lot. I wanted more than anything to be with him—be the woman he deserved to have at his side. He deserved someone who wasn't a mess like I was—someone who wasn't broken and had killed countless men and women.

It wasn't just what I went through with Sebastien —but what I had done with my own hands. He had no idea. He didn't know how I tortured people, how I brought in people to have their minds messed with, how I forced scientists to work for Bastien.

All of it was coming to the surface though, and he would see the truth—he would see how much of a monster I was. Then he would leave me, just like he should.

I sat up and stretched. I hated being locked away in a room like this—it brought up too many thoughts and feelings I didn't want to deal with. And part of me wished I had some morphine-B.

But I couldn't. I had gone through death, and the doctor said if I had it again, I wouldn't be able to wean off. It was on my chart that a doctor wasn't supposed to administer it but one of the other painkillers if need be. Hopefully it would never come to that.

As if I would ever not be injured again.

I didn't worry about a hospital administering it. But Bastien knew I was on it—and he knew I couldn't be back on it. While I'd never told him directly, I had a feeling he found out as he always did.

I felt a small shift in the ship. We were coming out of hyperspace, which meant we were nearing the border checkpoint. I wondered how Bastien was going to do it—how he was going to convince the border patrol, who would all have his photo under the most wanted man alive. He would either have to know someone, which was likely, or he would have a different plan that would get him through, probably involving me.

An hour passed, and I waited patiently. I was used to waiting. I was used to sitting with my thoughts. I had learned how to completely zone out, although many thoughts did sneak past more often than I wanted to acknowledge. Perhaps earlier I was more successful because I just dosed myself.

Part of me wished I could have another dose.

The door slid opened, and Bastien stood in the doorway. "*Guten morgen, meine Liebchen.* Did you have a good night's sleep?"

I glanced up at the light. "Sure. Just wish the

light would turn off at night, but other than that, it was just peachy."

He smiled. "I'll see to that. Now come with me. I need you to convince someone to act as if they are supposed to be here."

He meant Mary. The border patrol would be asking us all questions, so she would have to lie or at least act as if she chose to be here. That wasn't going to be easy—not after how she was when I saw her last. She was terrified, which I understood. Her life was in danger, and one of her friends had just lost her life because of me. I wouldn't want anyone to come near me after all that.

Especially Bastien.

I didn't want to be near him either, but I didn't get a choice. I had to go through with it, or he would make my life even worse.

I followed Bastien into the corridor. Walrum and two other soldiers were standing out there. I didn't know how I felt about Walrum being there. I thought I was used to seeing his face again, but I wasn't. I had to push back the tears—the anguish and fury I felt toward Bastien for what he'd done to him.

He wouldn't get away with this.

Bastien led us down the hall toward where Mary was being held. Walrum walked behind me, and I felt as if my skin were crawling. I didn't turn back to look at him, but I could feel him watching me. I still wasn't sure how he viewed me—if he understood who I used to be to him and who I was now to him.

Walrum had been my everything.

We came upon Mary's room, and Bastien turned to face me. "Now, what I want you and Mary to do is to pretend you are the cooks on this ship. I already have all the documentation needed, but I can't exactly explain why two of my cooks are locked away in their rooms, now can I? If I listed you as prisoners, they would have to go through some checks, and it will increase the risk of being discovered."

"So you want me to convince her to not freak out as she gets questioned by the border patrol?"

"And her life is on the line—be sure to include that."

"How would you even be convincing the border patrol? Your face is more than likely plastered everywhere."

He grinned devilishly. "I have my ways—don't worry about that. Simply worry about keeping your little friend alive."

I frowned as he opened the door. Bastien stepped out of the way and gestured so I could go inside. At least he wasn't going with me.

Mary was still huddled on the bed in the corner. Her eyes were red as if she had still been crying. I didn't know what to do or say to make her feel better. She wouldn't trust anything I had to say, and I didn't blame her.

I nodded to Bastien to close the door, and he did just that. I couldn't really talk to her woman to woman with him standing there or calm her down when I was also worried about him doing something. I knew there were cameras in here, but those were easier to ignore.

"Get away from me!" Mary yelled as she threw her pillow at me.

I sighed. "Mary, we are almost at the border.

Please listen to me."

"No! This is all your fault! You were the one who betrayed us! Because of you, Alexandra is dead!"

"It is and I wish more than anything that I could go back and save her, but I can't. I can, however, keep you safe. Now please listen to me."

"How can I trust you? How do I know you aren't going to lead me to my death?"

"If they wanted you dead, they would have already killed you. No, you are leverage to keep from acting out. If they keep you safe, they know I'll do as they say."

She shifted on the bed. "They are using me to keep you in line?"

I nodded. "*Jawohl.*"

"And if you do anything to make them mad, they are going to take it out on me? That doesn't seem fair."

"It's not, but that's how villains get what they want. I'll do everything though, to keep you safe. So please listen to me. Then I'll figure out how to get you out of here."

She let out a defeated laugh. "So you say that out

loud where they can hear you? That doesn't seem at all reassuring."

"It's no surprise that I'm trying to get out of here. Now will you listen to what I have to say?"

Mary hesitated but slowly nodded. "*Bene*, I'll hear you out."

"We are coming to the border. I'm not sure how, but Sebastien will manage to get to YamaXie. The two of us can't act like prisoners. We need to act as if we are the chefs. You get to be my assistant. Now"—I held out my hand—"come with me. We will get you cleaned up and whip something up. Maybe there are some ingredients for a yummy dessert that we can have later."

"How can he get past the border? None of this is fair."

"I know. But once we are in YamaXie, we can figure out what to do. We just need to be able to get there alive first."

She stood up. "Fine. I'll come with you. But I'm not forgiving you for what you did."

That was fine—I wouldn't forgive myself for what happened either.

CHAPTER VI

Nik

Well, Bardon wasn't happy that two of them snuck onto the ship and were now part of our mission. They were technically civilians and weren't supposed to be on missions such as this, although Bardon had been the one who had hired them in the first place. After everything they'd witnessed and were now dealing with, I couldn't really blame them for wanting to save their sister and girlfriend. I just wished I didn't have to deal with the fact I had to keep them safe as I searched for Rebecca.

Because when it came down to it, I didn't believe I could keep anyone safe—not even myself.

Sebastien didn't care to play fair, and he didn't care who he hurt. All he cared about was power and making people fear him. He needed to be stopped, no matter the cost.

We were always taught that the culprit had to be brought in for questioning. No one was supposed to take the law into their own hands but to allow the criminal to go through the judicial system. That, of course, didn't apply in incidences of someone attacking, and honestly, we were sent on assassination missions quite often. But when it came to someone who was in the military—someone who had done horrible things like Sebastien—they wanted them brought in so they could deliver the punishment. That way, families of those affected could feel they had a part of the trial.

But Sebastien didn't deserve that. No, he deserved a slow, painful death that was against the

Geneva Convention.

Did I care it was wrong? No—not after everything that had happened. Bardon had ordered us to bring him back in, but I doubted I could do that. After what he'd done to Rebecca, I couldn't let a monster like him live.

And that was going to be hard with Russ and Samuel tagging along. They would either get in my way or try to stop me, which I couldn't let happen. I wouldn't even let Jonathan stop me, which meant I would have to lose them somewhere along the way. Jonathan and I would be splitting if we didn't find anything at the border we checked first, so perhaps I could get him to take both Samuel and Russ.

As if that wouldn't look suspicious.

I got up from my cot and sighed as I slid the door open. The room was as large as they got. There was no point in having a whole bedroom for one to sleep in for a ship the size as this. I was used to sleeping in such a small room, as most of the military ships had rooms such as these while traveling. I had spent more nights sleeping in a cot than I did in an actual bedroom, which was odd to think about. It barely fit two people—that much I knew.

Jonathan and I both took a rest break since Samuel could fly the ship and Russ was a mechanic. But I couldn't sleep—there was too much on my mind. I headed toward the bathroom and splashed water on my face. I stared in the mirror at my graying blond hair. Was I really getting that old? It felt like just yesterday Jonathan, Walrum, and I had graduated from the academy and began our mission.

Except it wasn't just yesterday—it had been nearly two decades, and Walrum was no longer himself.

I had really thought Alexandra had fixed Walrum and he was back to his old self, but I was wrong. We were all fooled. Walrum was long gone and now was an empty shell, doing whatever the puppet master ordered. My best friend was gone—there was likely no way he was ever going to be fixed.

Placing my hand just under my eye, I felt the scar of the injury that had once taken my eyesight. After a few minor surgeries, I could see again. It was strange—I had gotten so used to having only one eye. Now I had almost my entire sight back. I could have gotten a few more surgeries to make it one hundred percent, but then everything had fallen apart.

There was a knock on the door.

"Do I even want to know what you're doing in there?" I heard Jonathan comment.

I chuckled and opened the door. "Sorry, was getting lost in my thoughts again."

"Hey, you don't have to lie. I don't judge. But you do have your own cot to do that in."

I punched him in the arm and stepped outside. "Did you need to use the restroom, or were you looking for me?"

"I was looking for you, actually. We were about to have dinner or lunch or breakfast. I'm not sure what time it is anymore."

That was common for military men who traveled a lot. I scratched the back of my neck.

"Sure, let me just change out of these sweats."

"No one is going to care if you're wearing

sweats. There're only four of us."

I shrugged. "Yeah, but I prefer to feel more official. Wakes me up and gets me going."

"Suit yourself. See you in a few."

I went back to my cot and changed out in the corridor. It was all men on the ship, and it was always awkward to try to change out and into clothes in the cot-sized room. After I finished, I headed to the dining area and kitchen.

The moment I stepped into the kitchen, I thought I saw Rebecca at the stove, only to realize it was Russ. They, of course, look nothing alike, but I had been so used to her making our meals that my mind decided to play a mean trick on me.

I needed to stop thinking about her and focus on the mission. I took a deep breath and sat down between Samuel and Jonathan.

"How far out are we from the border?"

Samuel answered. "About four hours. It won't be much longer now until we get some answers."

"Hopefully, at least."

Samuel shrugged. "I know it's a long shot to be at the correct border, but once we get into their mainframe, I'll be able to find them—trust me."

Jonathan pointed at him. "No illegal hacking."

"Then get permission. You are literally sleeping with one of the highest-ranking officers in the Nreff Nation. It shouldn't be a problem."

Jonathan let out a chuckle. "That doesn't mean he can do whatever he wants. He's not Admiral Wilde. He tries to do everything legally."

"And what's illegal about asking for all the information from the border when there's a criminal at large?" Russ asked as he set the food down.

I understood why Jonathan wasn't sure what meal it was. I had thought it was simply because time had no meaning in space, but I was wrong. It was because Russ had made hash browns, eggs, sausage, sandwiches, and fruit. Apparently he was hungry.

Jonathan answered the question I had completely forgotten he asked. "Because it interferes with rights of the other territory and people on transporters, *et patati et patata*. I'm just saying, don't get him in trouble."

"So you are saying don't get caught." Samuel smiled.

Jonathan pointed his fork at him and winked. "No, if you catch my drift."

We certainly hadn't done every mission by code. Sometimes code was wrong, and sometimes it got in the way of what we needed to do. Jonathan and I both understood that, but since we were the only two on the mission, we couldn't exactly say that to civilians.

"What are the odds of going to the right border?" Russ asked as he filled his plate with food.

I scratched my head. "Let's see, there's forty entrance points for the border… and that's if we are correct in thinking he is going to YamaXie, so a pretty low percentage, although we are going to one of the smaller ones that is less likely to check everything…" I shrugged as I took a bite of hash browns. "Hopefully it's higher than that then."

"So we would need to look at those records stat," Samuel added. "Otherwise we will never find them."

"Why can't we just search for them in YamaXie

and skip all this nonsense?"

"Because if we can figure out what ship they were in, we can find the manifest of where they are going and which planet they are heading to."

Samuel picked a few grapes and popped them into his mouth. "But couldn't he just lie on that?"

I sighed. "There is that… But we could get a better idea of what ship he has. When they left Regenwelt, they used more than one ship, so it made it harder for us to track. We will have to come for proof on which ship Sebastien is on."

Samuel shook his head. "He really did think of everything, didn't he?"

I nodded, as did Jonathan. Jonathan speared one of the sausages with his fork. "Now, let's eat up and prepare for the border."

CHAPTER VII

Rebecca

I did not miss going through border patrol.

That was mainly because every time I had to go through in the past few years, I had to sneak and pray I wouldn't be found out—mainly by Bastien. Now I was with him and had to get through this without messing up, which was easier said than done.

He had a few people he could threaten into helping him, and he had people in YamaXie who would fudge a few papers, but that didn't mean someone might notice us and report our whereabouts to the authorities.

Which was exactly what I was hoping for.

Nik would be on his way—Admiral Bardon was clever enough to know where Bastien would be heading. I just had to do something nonchalantly to alert Nik, but nothing big enough where Bastien would notice and take it out on Mary. The problem was, what could I do when he was breathing down my neck?

I had to put Mary's safety first, so it would only be something I could get away with. I glanced around as we stepped into the lobby of the border.

My anxiety began to increase. I didn't know why. If we were caught, then I wouldn't have to deal with Bastien any longer. Part of me knew that was a lie—part of me knew he would blame me and take it out on Mary if anything went wrong even if it wasn't my fault. As for Mary, she did her best to hide her fear, but I could feel her tremble next to me. I watched as she held herself tightly, even though we were simply chefs checking in. Once we finished our paperwork, we would head back inside and act as if we were simply doing what we were hired to do. Then after they checked the ship's manifest, we would be on our way.

Theoretically.

There was a list of people I knew had Bastien's back in this nation, so I wasn't sure what planet we would be heading to or if he would change ships eventually. That meant I couldn't point Nik in the right direction, but I could somehow let him know he was here.

Any accident or trip up I made as a distraction would be discovered quickly, so that wasn't going to be a choice. It would have to be swift and clever. I glanced up at the cameras. Even if there was footage of me here, it could take days, maybe even weeks for them to find it. There were multiple border patrols, and they wouldn't be sure what times to check, even with software combing through it. I had to do something a bit more noticeable.

I thought back on all the missions Nik and I had together and if there was any cue or check we made to each other if someone was in trouble. Nothing I could think of would be easy to do here.

As I kept on pondering, I felt a hand slip around my waist. It took every ounce of restraint I had not to flip Walrum over onto his back. That would have appeared suspicious and cause trouble for Bastien, which was not something I wanted to do at that moment.

"Hello, *Schätzchen*, waiting long?" Walrum smiled as if we were a couple.

I narrowed my eyes. "What? On the manifest, are we a couple or something?"

"Of course. Bastien said it was everything you ever wanted—you and me together."

Glancing over at Mary, who had stepped away from us, not wanting to be near Walrum, I reminded myself why I didn't just scream and alert the authorities right then and there. I had to keep her safe. Walrum didn't just come over to torment me—he also came over to be her guard.

"Right. Everything I have ever wanted."

"I honestly wonder what kind of man I would have been to be engaged to someone like you. I admit, you are quite attractive, but your hands are so red with blood." He grinned. "That's right—he never knew, did he?"

I bit my lip, not wanting to answer that. Because he was right—Walrum never knew my secret. If I told him, there was no way he would stay with me. I would be all alone.

That wasn't true for Nik, however. He knew the truth, but he thought I was innocent—he thought Bastien always moved my hand for me when that wasn't the case. Everything I had done was by my own free will—or at least it had been in the beginning. Then when I'd left him, he'd started to use more force and threaten me.

Perhaps I never did have a choice then—perhaps I was innocent.

Who was I kidding? I could have put up more of a fight. I could have told someone and figured out a way to escape. I was killing and torturing people for him. I was as much at fault as he was. After a while, I knew I couldn't run or else I would also be charged with the same crimes.

Just like now.

We made it to the front of the line and gave the officers our fake cards. I prayed that whoever Bastien had hired were better than the guards I had used when Nik and I were in hiding. On some planets, the IDs didn't work and we had to run for it. Luckily the officers never caught us, but I knew our location was put on Bastien's radar, and we had to move quickly. I was never afraid of being arrested and tried for what we were set up for. I was afraid of what Bastien would do to me.

And yet here I was—helping him get across the border.

The officer looked over the screen he had after I scanned in. Finally he nodded at the both of us. "You two are good to go."

That was surprisingly easy. "Thank you," I said as I grabbed our scan cards. I stepped to the side so Mary could scan in.

Her hands were trembling. She didn't say a word as she handed over the scan card and the officer looked at her details.

"You are good to go as well."

Mary joined us as we headed back toward the ship. I peered around. This was my last chance. I had to do something.

There were a few businesses on our way back to the ship. My stomach grumbled, and I realized that could be my chance.

"Walrum, why don't we grab something to eat?"

"Aren't you a cook? We should just head straight back to the ship."

"But the food here smells so good. Don't you think?"

His stomach answered for him. The Walrum I knew couldn't say no to food, and I prayed his body would remember that.

He glanced over at the Italian restaurant. "Fine, but it better be quick and no funny business."

I smiled as I turned to Mary. "Come on—let's go get some food."

We entered the small restaurant. It was jam-packed with people, which was perfect for me. I would just have to be clever about this and pray that Nik did, in fact, search the right border first. It wouldn't matter what kind of clue I made if they weren't here.

The line moved fairly quickly, and we got to the front. I ordered some spaghetti and marinara, and Walrum ordered a lasagna. Mary at first wasn't going to order anything, but the thought of Italian food made her change her mind. We also grabbed a couple of to-go cups for drinks. I handed mine to Walrum.

"Can you get me a root beer?"

He narrowed his eyes. "And where will you be?"

I shrugged. "Waiting here for our food. Sometimes these places are fast and I don't want anyone else to grab it, otherwise we will have to make Bastien wait even longer for us."

He frowned but did as I asked. I turned back to the clerk. "Can you do me a favor?"

"What is it?"

"I know you get a lot of people through here, but if you see a tall blond man about my age and a scar over one of his eyes who is searching for something, can you give him a message? He may be with a man with curly dark hair and a scruffy face."

She appeared confused. "Um, I don't know…"

"Please? He and I are playing a fun game, and I don't know how else to leave a clue."

She sighed. "Sure, I guess. What is the clue?"

"Can you just tell him 'ciao'?"

"You mean like the name of this restaurant?"

I nodded. "Exactly. And if you finish your shift before he shows, can you let someone else know? Pretty please?"

She shrugged. "Yeah, sure." She turned and grabbed the to-go bag that had just been delivered. "And I believe this is yours. Have a nice day!"

"You too."

I grabbed the bag and prayed that Nik would end up here and not somewhere else. For once, I wanted luck to be on my side.

"You got the food?" Walrum asked as he stepped up behind me, making me jump a little.

I nodded. "Yup. We are good to go."

Mary joined us with her drink. She kept her eyes away from Walrum and followed me as we headed back to the ship. I knew I was going to be questioned about this, but I had to do it—I had to leave him a note to know I was, in fact, here.

It was our only chance. Then he could take Mary and I could make the final blow against Bastien.

CHAPTER VIII

Nik

We were at the border.

I glanced out at all the ships. There were hundreds, and this was only one of around forty border checkpoints that Sebastien could have gone —and that was if he went to YamaXie and not one of the other two nations. And, again, that was only if he tried leaving the nation.

There were too many what-ifs in this scenario for me. I just wanted to find the bastard and kill him so I didn't have to worry about Rebecca any longer.

Jonathan would fight me on that, however. Bardon wanted him back in prison where he could rot, but I didn't think that was a good idea. There were too many people who feared him and would do as he said. He needed to be killed at this point.

I felt a hand on my shoulder. "I don't think you have to worry. Rebecca is strong and won't let him break her."

I didn't believe that—or at least it didn't have anything to do with her being strong or not. No one should have to deal with what she was facing, not to mention he was using Mary as leverage. Who knew what he would be able to get her to do for him as he threatened Mary's life.

"I think we just need to get this over with. And pray this is the way he went."

"It will take some time to get them to give us the information we need, not to mention if this isn't it, we will have to get even more paperwork to check the other borders."

I nodded. "I know. And they don't like to be questioned even though we all know they let criminals pass through the border constantly."

He let out a brief sigh. "You're telling me. You and I got over the border quite easily, didn't we?"

It was true—Rebecca and I were able to travel between borders without a problem, although they never went back to Nreff Nation just to be on the safe side. As for Jonathan, he was able to make it to the Regit Republic, and then they were able to get back into the Nreff Nation without a hitch. Rebecca was only caught because someone alerted them.

So, in other words, the border points were pointless. But at least they could, hopefully, get the okay to check through their information.

Samuel docked the ship, and they all went through the checkpoint with ease, which wasn't a surprise. If Sebastien had already made it through here, then we, who had no alerts against us, shouldn't have a problem.

If Rebecca had made her way through here, then she would have tried to leave a clue. As to what sort of clue she would have been able to leave, I had no idea. I glanced around as we headed toward the office of the admiral in charge of this station.

"Did Bardon already alert them we were coming?" I asked.

Jonathan nodded his head slowly. "*Oui*, he did…"

"But they are being assholes about it, aren't they?"

"They want a warrant."

I sighed. "Is Bardon trying to get a warrant?"

"Yup, but it will be another day."

I shook my head. I couldn't believe this was happening. Were they idiots? Was everyone in politics and the military just idiots with ego complexes? I knew the answer to that was yes, but it was still beyond frustrating. There was a lot at stake, especially with the peace treaties coming up. If Bastien had his way, which appeared more likely with each and every moment, there would be a war.

It was as if most of the men in power wanted it to happen. It was as if they didn't think safety was fun and wanted to actually attack for more resources even though no nation was suffering. There was no reason for war—not with how large each nation was and how many planets each of them had. So what was the point? Why couldn't everyone just get along?

We came upon the office of the admiral, and the guards on duty stopped us.

"Where do you think you two are going?" the guard asked.

Jonathan flashed his ID. "I am Captain Jonathan Dupont of the Nreff Nation. Admiral Yarnell knows we are coming."

The guard went into the room and spoke with the admiral. I took in a deep breath and let it out slowly. I had a feeling this wasn't going to go how I wanted it to. I had to be careful not to punch someone in the face.

Coming back out from the office, the guard gestured for us to enter. We nodded and went inside.

The office was similar to all the other offices that admirals had in the military. It was plain with a mix of paper and screens, a very frustrated-looking admiral on the other side of a desk.

Admiral Yarnell was tapping his finger on the table as if not wanting to deal with us. Both Jonathan and I saluted.

He waved at us. "At ease. What are you here for?"

This was not going to go well, I could feel it. Jonathan answered, knowing I would probably start shouting. "We are here to look through video footage and scans from ID cards. I believe Admiral Bardon talked to you about it."

He leaned back and folded his arms. "He did. And I told him we were on the lookout for Admiral Wilde, so he didn't need to send anyone here."

I clenched my fist, and Jonathan smacked my hand without turning his attention away from the admiral.

"Yes, we know that, but extra eyes will always help the search—"

"Look, I don't have time to deal with the likes of you. Either Admiral Bardon needs to get a warrant or he needs to mind his own business. I'm busy, now leave."

Jonathan began to turn, but I shook my head.

"No, you can't be serious. We are here to help you. There is a wanted criminal who has escaped from a military base, and we are pretty sure he came this way. You're telling us we need to get a warrant?"

Admiral Yarnell stood up. "I beg your pardon?"

I was about to go on when Jonathan put his hand over my mouth. "He didn't mean that. We will be leaving."

The admiral glared at us as Jonathan dragged me out of the room. Once we left the room, Jonathan let go of my mouth.

"Are you trying to get us arrested? You know if we don't wait for the warrant, he'll just cause more problems for us."

I shook my head. "I'm just tired of all this bureaucracy. He is causing us not to be able to find Sebastien and Rebecca. He knows he's at fault—he knows all the borders are corrupt and he can easily pass. He just doesn't want us to find out how truly corrupt it is."

"You are right—which is why we need to wait for that warrant."

I shook my head. "And what if Bardon doesn't

get it? How will we find them then?"

Jonathan shrugged. "We will just have to start searching planets, or perhaps Rebecca will be able to get away and get a message. We just have to be patient."

"Easy for you to say," I shot back. "The love of your life isn't in the hands of some psychotic killer."

He frowned. "No, but for years he caused me not to be able to be with the man I love. We all have faced horrible things because of that man. Stop being impatient. We are doing everything we can, and we have to make sure we have a clear head or else it could all be for nothing."

He had a point there. I let out a breath. "I'm sorry you dealt with that. She was just… I don't know. I just want this all to be over."

"I know, and it will be soon enough. As long as we do this by the book."

I wanted to say that wasn't true—how we had been doing it by the book for years and that hadn't gotten us anywhere. It was when we did things how we wanted to that we actually caught him—when we had used Rebecca to draw him out.

And I felt horrible about agreeing to that.

I turned to the exit. "We should go find the others. They are probably wondering what we're up to."

Jonathan nodded, and we headed back out to the main area. Samuel and Russ were waiting for us where we left them—sitting in the waiting and lounge area. They stood up when they saw us.

"What did they say?" Samuel asked.

I shook my head. "They won't budge until the warrant goes through, if it does."

Samuel leaned in and whispered to me, "Just find me a computer."

Jonathan pointed at him. "No. We are not taking shortcuts. We are figuring this out legally or else it will cause us more problems."

Samuel frowned but winked at me when Jonathan wasn't looking. Was I going to go against my best friend's wishes and hack into this place's cameras? I knew I shouldn't, but the fact that we had someone here who could do that wasn't helping my moral compass.

As we stood there, I smelled something tasty. I turned to find an Italian restaurant called Ciao. Italian food sounded great right about now.

"Let's get some food," I said. "I'm starving."

Russ took a deep inhale. "Whatever that is, it smells like some good food. I'm in."

Samuel and Jonathan nodded, and we headed toward the restaurant. It was crowded, but Russ was able to grab us a table.

"What do you all want?" I asked as I stood up.

Russ was quick to answer. "Alfredo please!"

"I'll take a lasagna," Samuel said.

Jonathan stood up. "I'll come with you. I have the credit card to put this on the military's dime." He winked.

I laughed as I followed him to the cashier. The moment we got to the front of the line, the cashier pointed at me. "Hey, you don't happen to be named Nik?"

I froze. Why would a cashier at a random border checkpoint know that? "I am. Why do you ask?"

"There was a woman here yesterday who asked me to give you a message. I was disappointed you didn't come by yesterday but glad you didn't come when I wasn't on shift. I wasn't sure if any of the others would remember to tell you."

My heart was beginning to race. A woman? Was it Rebecca? "What was the message?"

"She said to just say ciao. Not much of a message, but she said you would understand."

My eyes widened. It was Rebecca—she had been here. We'd picked the correct border checkpoint.

We were right on their tail.

CHAPTER IX

Rebecca

His hand slapped me straight in the face. I didn't wince but felt the bite linger for longer than I had remembered it from the other times I had been slapped by him. Perhaps he had more practice.

"What did you say to that cashier?" Bastien questioned.

I shook my head. "Thank you? I just grabbed my

food, told her thank you, and we came back here."

"I know you are lying—I know you gave her some message."

"And then what?" I laughed. "Who would she tell? What information would I be able to give anyone?"

He slapped me again. "Knowing you—probably something to ruin all my plans."

I wiped the blood off my lip. I was back in my room, under surveillance after the so-called scene I had caused. No one had any proof, and Bastien didn't stay around long enough to find out, as he didn't want anyone snooping around and finding the truth.

"If I had told them who you were, they would have stopped us. I don't know where we are going, so I couldn't have told them that either. Walrum, or whoever he is now, doesn't know what he's talking about. He's crazy and suspicious since you played with his brain."

Bastien raised his hand again, and I flinched. He grinned at that and lowered his hand. "What were you doing grabbing food? You knew we needed to leave right away."

"Which was why I had him get drinks while I waited for the food—I didn't want anyone else to grab it or else we would have taken longer and you would have been even more furious with us."

Bastien's lip tilted up. "Well, at least you were thinking about me a little bit."

"Less thinking and more worrying about my own skin."

He grabbed my chin and forced me to look straight into his eyes. "The one thing I hate most about how well I taught you is that you are a master at lying now. I should have never taught you how to lie to me, *meine Liebchen*. You were too good of a student."

I didn't say anything but glared at him. He had a point—I was good at lying because of him. It was one of the things I was thankful he taught me because I knew I could use it on him.

Bastien let out a breath as he let go of my jaw. "I'm just not sure what to do. You told her something—I know you did. You are too clever not to pull something."

"And as I said—I told her thank you. I know it's a hard concept, but people can be polite to one another."

He slapped me again. I smiled a little, as I knew I deserved that one.

"How about I bring Mary in here? Would you talk if her life was being threatened?"

I rolled my eyes. "Would you stoop so low as to hurt a kid? For no good reason? I didn't tell her anything. Again, what would a cashier do? They didn't alert the authorities you were here. I don't know where you are going, so there isn't any info I can give."

He sat down on my bed and rubbed his chin. "Perhaps. But you are being very specific as if you thought this through."

I rolled my eyes. "Can you just leave me alone? It's been a day. I didn't do anything. I just wanted some food."

"Were there eggs in those noodles?" he asked.

I blinked. "Excuse me?"

"You are a vegan, for some odd reason, and always check to see if the noodles have eggs in them. So did you this time?"

I hadn't. I needed to get my message across and didn't want to go anywhere else. I knew Nik—I knew he loved Italian food and would go there. Not to mention the name of the restaurant was the same as the code we had in place.

"I— Yeah, I did. They didn't use eggs."

He stood back up and grabbed my jaw. With a smile I knew meant business, he looked straight into my eyes. "That was a lie. Now, are you going to be a good girl and tell me the truth?"

Well, I was fucked. If I told him the truth, he was going to beat me. If I told him a lie, he was going to beat me until I told the truth.

"Fine. I told her to tell Nik something."

He glared at me. "What did you tell her?"

"Nothing specific, I assure you. I didn't have time. I told her to be on the lookout for a man with a scar through his eye. He went by the name of Nik and to tell him *ciao*."

Bastien shook his head. "I don't follow."

"Ciao was code for if something was wrong."

"That's it?"

I shrugged. "It would be enough to tell him where I was and where to start looking. But since I don't know where we are going and I have a feeling you have a fake route in place, that isn't going to give him much to work off of, now is it?"

Bastien stood there silent for a moment. I feared he was going to snap, and I flinched as he started laughing.

"Oh, my dear *Liebchen*, how you make these games all the more exciting." He ruffled my hair and left me sitting in my prison cell, alone.

What the hell was that? Why did he laugh and leave me? I took a deep breath as I headed toward the bathroom. My cheeks burned, and I used some cool water to try to help the swelling. It didn't do much.

Bastien knew Nik would come for me. Did he have something planned? Was he going to set a trap for him? The odds of Nik finding my message were slim to none, not to mention the stupidity when it came to the border officers working with the rest of the military. They might not even get footage from them—especially if they were in with Bastien.

But I had to hope—I needed Nik to find me so he could take Mary and I could be free of the burden that was keeping her safe. Then I could end it all, as long as Bastien didn't end everything I cared about first.

I whimpered as I climbed into the shower and turned the water on. I didn't bother to take my clothes off—I didn't care. I just wanted somewhere to cry where I knew there were no cameras and people watching.

I felt the ship shift out of hyperspace. We had arrived at a planet. I wondered if we were going to swap ships or if we were going to stay planet-side. There were a lot of places to hide on a planet, but that wasn't exactly what Bastien wanted—he wanted to start a war.

And for what? To gain some money? I had a feeling that wasn't exactly it. He had money—my guess was he wanted the pleasure of looking out at all the chaos and knowing he was behind it all. I had to admit, there was definitely unrest between the nations. Nik and I had seen it when we were on the run. It didn't make sense, however, as there was no need to expand—all the nations had enough resources and land. The only reason they would want to do it was out of pure chaos and power.

Which I wouldn't put past any of those men and women in charge.

I knew I would be leaving the military as soon as I could, not that I was technically in it any longer. I only chose this because it was my only option to get away from my parents. Had I known it would lead to this, well, perhaps I would have stuck it out or had simply run away. Who knew what would have happened with Bastien and the others if that were the case.

Getting up, I changed into some new clothes and waited for someone to come get me. The ship jerked a little as it docked with the spaceport.

With a couple of days having gone by, I had an idea which planet we were near. It was New Tokyo, one of the closest planets to the border. I was rusty with my Japanese but had a feeling I would need to practice—if I was let out of my prison, that is. It was a high possibility that Bastien would simply throw me in another cell and use me as leverage against Bardon.

I didn't like being used.

The door slid open. I was surprised to find it wasn't Bastien but Walrum.

"What do you want? Are we on port?"

He nodded. "We are."

"Where is Bastien?"

"Why? Do you miss him already?"

"Nein. I just like knowing where that *Schwein* is so I don't have to worry."

He laughed. "Well, he's busy dealing with security. He apparently knows some people at the port, and they are hesitant to accept his help."

"I would be too if someone who was wanted for crimes against humanity was saying he could help them."

Walrum shrugged. "I think he'll be able to persuade them. As for you—I need to get you off the ship with Mary and head down to the planet."

"Where a new cell awaits?" I asked as we stepped out into the corridor.

"We wouldn't have it any other way."

It was strange talking to him like this. In some ways, he still had Walrum's humor—his laughter— but he didn't have any sort of humanity left in him. His stomach still growled for Italian food like it used to, and I was able to use that against him. But he reported that I talked to the cashier, so he still was on Bastien's side. I couldn't trust him even though he used to be the one person I had trusted the most.

Besides Nik.

We made it to Mary's cell, and she didn't put up much of a fuss, leaving it like she had earlier. She understood what position we were in and that she needed to comply if she wanted to stay safe.

The three of us didn't say much as we headed into the port. The port was much the same as every other port, other than the signs were in Japanese and Chinese characters. I could at least read them, but by the looks on Walrum's and Mary's faces, they could not.

"Where are we supposed to be heading?" I asked. "I can read the signs."

"We are to be heading down to the planet, so

whatever points that way."

That was easy enough, although I was surprised that we weren't to wait for Bastien to take us down. After what had happened at the port, I wouldn't have expected him to want me out of his sight.

Unless this was a test.

I didn't have another way of getting a message to Nik—especially since he didn't speak Japanese or Chinese. I glanced around for a camera. At least he would have that access eventually. Hopefully. It was a different territory after all.

We made it to the transport down, and I stared out at the stars. The universe was so vast and yet so small in a way. Humans kept expanding into it, think they controlled everything—thinking they could have more power than the gods themselves.

Just like Bastien thought. And I wanted to be there when he saw his ivory tower come crashing down.

CHAPTER X

Nik

Rebecca had been at this border checkpoint. She was nearby.

We were only behind a day, but the time between them and Bastien was growing with each minute that passed. We needed access to the cameras and all the people who had gone through here, but the officials weren't letting us have it.

I paced back and forth on our ship as it was still docked at the port. We could stay here for as long as we wanted, as long as we paid the fees. I didn't want to stay that long, however, as we were so close. We knew around what time they had been here so we wouldn't have to go through as much data as we would have going in blind.

"Nik, you need to stop pacing. You're making me tired," Jonathan commented.

I stopped and turned to him. "We know she was here, and we know around what time to go through cameras and IDs, and yet we have to wait for a warrant that may or may not go through. This is ridiculous, Jonathan, and you know it."

Jonathan shrugged. "I don't know what to tell you other than you could try to ask the admiral on the YamaXie side of the checkpoint. I have a feeling they would be even less welcoming to a military officer wanting to sift through the data."

He had a point there—the officers in other nations weren't going to be welcoming, especially since it was a mess within our government, not theirs. Once we did make it over to the other side to search for them, they were going to cause a lot of trouble for us, so we would have to work on the down low. I wasn't sure how that was going to play out since Bastien could use that against us. He was loved by some of their officials, always had been. I had a feeling they were going to hide him as well.

If it weren't for the fact that he had Rebecca and Mary, I wasn't sure if I would have even cared at that point. A rotten apple could destroy a whole barrel, and it was apparent that the entire system needed to be tossed. If so many officials were willing to side with him, out of fear or not, then this war wouldn't be stopped. They all wanted it, and we would all be paying the consequences of that.

"Have you all gone back to the admiral and told them what the cashier at the restaurant said? Perhaps he would listen to you after that," Samuel suggested.

Both Jonathan and I laughed. Jonathan answered, "No, that's not something he would care about. He made that clear. He is going to go wait it out until Jacques sends over the warrant."

"When will that be?" Russ asked.

Jonathan shrugged. "Any time from now to a few days."

"And by then, Bastien could be anywhere," I muttered.

"But we will find him." Jonathan eyed me. "Because Rebecca never stays quiet. She tends to make a scene."

That was a fact. She got into fights all the time. I had a feeling if it weren't for Mary, she would have alerted the authorities as soon as they made it to the port, not caring if she would pay the price for that. But with Mary there, she couldn't do anything, which also meant she wouldn't be making any big scenes anytime soon.

I sat down and rubbed my face with my hands. This was entirely unfair. Why couldn't this be easy? Why couldn't our plan to stop him at the trial have gone smoothly? Why were so many people helping him?

Glancing over at Samuel, I wondered if he could do it—I wondered if he could hack into the computer system and get the information we needed. Then the two of us could head out after him and Jonathan could stay here as if we're waiting for the warrant. That way we could get a head start, and if anyone asked, we had all the official paperwork to get the information we needed. No one needed to know how we actually got the information—just that we had followed procedure.

But what if the warrant didn't go through? What if we weren't supposed to have the information? We could say it was luck since Rebecca left that message. She must have not known where they were going or else she would have left that in the message. She was doing well enough to get that info across, so at least there was that. But if Sebastien found out what she did, then she might be punished.

I felt a knot in my gut. How could he hurt her like he had all these years? How could he have tortured and killed all those people?

Because he was a psychopath. They all knew that going into this. But seeing how he snapped at Admiral Dr. Jørgensen shined more of a light on how he could change. When they worked with him, he seemed completely normal. If it hadn't been for Bardon, I doubted I would have ever been able to notice.

"If there is any shopping you need to do or if you want to hang out in the port, feel free to do so. We all just need to meet back here at…" Jonathan checked his watch. "Let's say 2000 hours."

All of us nodded, and I got up to leave the ship. I didn't particularly want to stay in this cramped place even if there were fewer people than the port.

But mainly I wanted to follow Samuel and see what he was up to and whether I could convince him to look for Rebecca and Mary.

Samuel was quick to try to lose everyone, which led me to believe he was going to hack this place's computers with or without anyone's help. If it weren't for the fact I was determined and wanted to know as well, he would have easily lost me.

But I tailed him at a far enough distance where he didn't notice. He weaved between people and headed toward the office area.

This was not going to end well if we got caught. Jonathan would be furious—he would say I had jeopardized everything because I wasn't being patient, which I admitted was partially true. But he also needed to realize that Bastien was clever, and if we waited for everything, which he was more than likely counting on, we would lose him. It had taken years for us to get this close—we couldn't give up because of some paperwork.

Samuel entered a storage closet, and I quickly followed. He jumped as I opened the door.

"It's not what it looks like."

I laughed. "Oh really? Because it looks like you snuck in here to crawl through the vents over to the next room to hack into a computer."

He shrugged. "Okay, it is what it looks like. But I can't wait any longer—I need to find Mary."

"I'm not here to stop you." I held out my arms. "Here, I'll give you a boost."

Samuel smiled. "I like you."

I helped him up to the vents and climbed in myself. Sure enough, the room next over was vacant and had a computer. Samuel cracked his knuckles as he got to work. I went over to the door and jammed the lock.

"That should buy us some time if anyone comes back. Hopefully they won't and I can fix it and none will be the wiser."

"Don't jinx it."

I stepped up behind him. "Sorry, I usually do."

"Great…"

He typed on the keyboard, and soon enough hundreds of videos popped up on the screen.

"That was fast."

Samuel shrugged. "Yeah, well, when you've been doing this your whole life…"

"I'll pretend I didn't hear that."

"As if all you've done with your life has been legal."

He had me there. He kept on typing, and I watched as people on top of people flashed on the screen. I kept my eyes out for Rebecca, but I didn't see her anywhere.

"Is this near the Italian restaurant?"

He nodded. "Yup. So far I don't see…" He pointed. "Wait! There! I see Mary."

I searched the screen and found Rebecca. My heart felt as if it had been stabbed. Walrum was with her—his arm wrapped around her like he was still her fiancé. He was whispering into her ear.

He was taunting her. I could tell. He wasn't the same Walrum we once knew—he had been brainwashed and did whatever Sebastien told him.

"What's the time stamp?" I asked.

Samuel searched the screen. "Yesterday, fourteen twenty-three."

I nodded. "Okay, can you back it up and see when they scanned their IDs? Then from there, we can get the ship info and the manifest of where they are headed."

"You don't have to tell me how to hack."

"Sorry, habit. I'm used to giving orders."

Samuel backed it up, and we watched as Walrum, Rebecca, and Mary all checked in together. I wasn't sure where Sebastien was—probably having tea with some official or something.

"Thirteen forty-eight. Remember that."

I nodded and repeated the numbers. Samuel did some typing and eventually pulled up the info of all those who had scanned their IDs to go across the border. He scrolled to the time stamp.

He pointed. "Here—thirteen forty-eight. Three people from the same ship scanned in at that kiosk. It says they are all cooks."

"That's them. I'm sure of it."

"Okay, looks like they were on a Nreff Nation multipassenger cruiser and were headed to… New Tokyo."

That wasn't too far from here. We were in luck—as long as they weren't just abandoning the ship there and finding a new one. Either way, we had the ship's info and could find them.

We were one step closer.

The door tried to slide open, and I heard talking on the other side. Samuel and I both stared at the door for a second, then clicked out of everything. As quickly as we could, we headed over to the vent and climbed back in. Closing it, we hurried to the storage room. Luckily, no one was in there searching and we made it out.

"You remembered to scramble the video of us in there, right?" I asked as we entered the corridor.

"Of course. I have made it this far in life—who do you think I am?"

"Just checking." I sighed as we rounded the corner.

And there stood Jonathan, his arms crossed in front of his chest. He glared at us, as if he knew what we had done.

"Schiße."

CHAPTER XI

Rebecca

"Do you really not remember anything?" I asked Walrum.

He had already taken Mary to her room and was setting up my own. At least this time I had a window—even if it was forty stories up. There was no way I could escape from it, and Bastien knew I wouldn't leave if he had Mary, who was on a completely different level. It was a nice room, I had to admit. I always appreciated the YamaXie culture and how they used color and minimalistic things to make a room have a beautiful appearance—a great contrast to the drab gray of the Nreff Nation.

Walrum shook his head. "I don't remember you or anything, just what I'm told."

"And how does that make you feel? Knowing your memories have been stolen?"

He hesitated. "I don't care. I'm not meant to care. If I cared, then I wouldn't be able to keep on going. Besides, why would you even ask that?"

I shrugged. "You and I used to be together. Pardon if I'm not curious as to what happens to my fiancé."

He looked away. "I... I don't remember that time. I know almost everything that happened—everything with Admiral Bardon and Jonathan and Nik... But it is like reading a story about someone else. I have no connections or feelings about any of it."

It was clear no one had asked him before. I knew that Alexandra had asked him questions, but perhaps she never asked him how he felt about it all. There were so many questions I still had—so many feelings that were inside me that I didn't want to address—but I didn't know what to do with the person who stood in front of me. He couldn't answer them because he was no longer that man. My Walrum was dead, and there was no way he could be brought back.

"I should be going. Sebastien should be back soon."

"Right. Him. I don't know how you could serve someone you know did this to you."

He turned to face me. "You aren't able to play mind tricks with me! I won't turn on him! Besides, you are one to talk. Aren't you the one who used to serve him and torture people? Aren't you as equally at fault as he is?"

Walrum had me there. "I did do many things I regret. I'll pay for my crimes. I know that to be a fact. But I didn't have my brain tampered with—or at least not medically. I was just wondering what it was like, that's all."

He frowned. "Well, it doesn't mean anything. I

take his orders, and I execute them. It's as simple as that."

"I suppose it is."

"What's that supposed to mean?"

I shrugged. "I just don't know what I would have done in your shoes. You could have told Alexandra the truth—you could have had your brain actually fixed and remembered everything. You could have gone back to being my Walrum. But instead, you went along with a crazed criminal. I just was curious what the thought process was there."

As I watched him, it was clear he never had those thoughts before, and he didn't know how to handle them. Up to then he had been taking orders, just as Sebastien created him to do. No one had questioned him—truly—and he was starting to realize what was wrong with him.

Which was why brainwashing was not the way to make an army. Even I knew that.

I stepped forward and placed my hand on his chest. "It saddens me to think you don't remember our life together and that it all was stopped short because of what Bastien had done. We could have retired, found a home near the lakeside, and lived our life how we wanted it. Instead, we are here: one of us remembering none of it and the other a hostage."

He backed away and turned to the door. "I have work to do." With that, he closed the door behind himself.

Well, those seeds were planted. I didn't know if it would work—if I could get him on my side or if I could at least use him to escape. I just needed to try a few more things to test it out.

I didn't like using him—I didn't like having to face him after everything that had happened. He had been the love of my life. It was bad enough having suffered through his death—this was much worse.

And yet it still made me feel guilty that I was in love with Nik.

Shaking the thoughts away, I went to the window and stared down at the city. There was definitely no way I could jump out of here. It was nice being able to see the view, however.

It was nearing the midafternoon, and the sun still

shone through the clouds onto the city. Flying cars traveled through the air—taking people from building to building. I wondered if Bastien would be back anytime soon or if he would let me think about what I had done for a bit. I hoped it was the latter.

I had nothing to do, which always was the worst. The bed at least appeared to be soft. Wherever we were—it was not a cheap place. I wondered if it was part of the YamaXie's military buildings or if they were just paying for us to stay here. Perhaps it was just a hotel and I didn't actually have a guard outside. I didn't feel like testing this theory quite yet, however.

Sitting down on the couch, I clicked on the television. At least I had that to keep me company, not to mention I could watch the news to see what exactly was going on in this city and what was happening with the treaty, if they were even reporting that.

The news was in Japanese on some stations and Mandarin on others. I could understand both, so it wasn't hard for me to figure out what was going on. Nothing about the treaty was being reported, and from what I could tell, there were no warnings out about Sebastien or me. He had made it through the border and onto the planet without raising an eyebrow.

Just my luck.

A few hours passed, and there was a knock on my door before it slid open. In stepped Bastien. I didn't bother getting up from the couch.

"Enjoying your room, I see," he commented.

I shrugged. "Just catching up on the news and watched a few anime shows. There's a lot of them out there."

"There are. Find out anything interesting on the news?"

I shook my head. "Nope. It doesn't seem you alerted any authorities you were here, or if you did they just didn't care. Proves to me that the entire universe is corrupted and will let any psychopath ruin democracy."

He smiled coldly. "You don't mean that."

"Why are you here?" I didn't want to argue any

longer. It wouldn't get anywhere.

"I have come to invite you to dinner. I found a place serving vegan sushi. What do you say?"

Sushi did sound good, but I didn't particularly want to go out with him. "I think I'll pass."

"That wasn't entirely a question."

"Then stop phrasing it like one."

It was taking everything for him not to slap me again—I could tell. "Just go get ready and change. There're a few dresses I have picked out for you in your closet. I'll wait in here."

I let out a brief sigh as I got up to see what he chose for me. To my surprise, they weren't as skimpy as I thought they would be. I didn't find anything wrong about showing skin, but I didn't want him seeing me in a dress like that. I grabbed the green Chinese-style dress and put it on. I pulled my hair back in a loose bun but didn't bother to put any makeup on, even though he had left some out for me. I really didn't care to look pretty, whatever that meant.

He glanced over at me. "Do your face as well. We are going out with officials."

I should have figured. I was arm candy. I would have to spend the entire night, smiling and pretending I was with him. I did not want to go through with this—mostly because I knew I was going to fuck it up and he was going to get mad at me.

As quickly as I could, I put on some light makeup that would be enough for Bastien to be happy with. I stepped out of the bathroom and smiled. "Happy now?"

"*Jawohl*. I get to have dinner with my favorite person in the whole world."

I held back a gag as he wrapped his arm around me and led me outside. Sure enough, there was a guard outside. I tried to act as if I were following him, but at the same time I was scoping out the area. It was clear, although they were nice quarters, it was not going to be easy to escape from here. I would have to find a different way of getting out of here—one that didn't involve getting shot or caught and tortured.

What great fun that would be.

CHAPTER XII

Nik

"You know how much trouble you are in, right? There is no way they aren't going to find out it was us?" Jonathan whispered as we made our way back to the ship.

"You didn't have anything to do with it—why are you so worried?"

"Because you literally broke into a military office

and hacked into their computer. You'll go to jail, and I could too because now I know what you did."

I rubbed my face. "Then how about we just leave now? Then we don't have to worry about it."

Jonathan took a deep breath, knowing he couldn't make a scene. "Then we would never be able to cross this border again."

"Clearly we could since Sebastien would be able to."

"No, because Sebastien doesn't piss off people he needs things from."

He had a point there. Sebastien knew when to play his cards right to get what he wanted. I let out a sigh. "I don't know what to tell you, Jonathan. I just needed to know where they went. I don't see the harm in it since we are hunting down a man who has killed and tortured hundreds of people. How is what we are doing wrong? Please explain it to me."

"Because if we do anything illegal, they will throw out his case and we will walk free. You do realize that, right?"

"And that is the stupidest shit I have ever heard.

Can we just admit that this whole thing is stupid and go in and just kill him?"

Jonathan stopped and turned to me. "You don't plan on murdering him, do you?"

"No?"

"Nik…"

"We have gone and executed plenty of people through the years," I whispered. "We have been amused and killed all those men in the woods not even a month ago. Are you trying to tell me he doesn't deserve to be assassinated? There are plenty of men we were hired to assassinate that were far, far worse than him."

"But that wasn't our orders."

"I don't give a rat's ass. He clearly can't be kept in a prison. What, do you think the trial will go smoother the second time around? No, it won't. None of this will be over until he is dead."

Jonathan turned and marched toward the ship, not saying a word. I had a feeling this conversation wasn't over, however.

Samuel trailed behind, his head down, as if he were a puppy caught doing something bad. I patted his back. "It's okay. I'll take the blame for this."

"It's not that—I just can't believe I got caught. I never get caught. This is a blow to my self-esteem."

I rolled my eyes. I should have figured. He turned to me. "So, when are we going to sneak away and get a ship to head to the planet?"

"Shh, don't stay that so loud that Jonathan can hear us."

"But that is what we are doing, correct?" he asked in a whisper.

I nodded. "It is. But we can't let Jonathan know. Tomorrow at 0400 hours, you and I will find us a ship and we'll head down."

"What about Russ?"

"Let's leave him with Jonathan. He's young and I don't want him to be there when shit goes down."

"But you don't mind me there when shit goes down."

"No, you are going to use your computer techniques to make sure shit doesn't go down. You understand?"

"That sounds like a plan to me."

I smiled as we followed Jonathan all the way to the ship. So far no alarms went off—no searches were happening. They didn't seem to know what had happened. I wasn't sure how Samuel hid us from the cameras, but whatever he did worked. The way I jammed the lock would have just appeared as a malfunction, so if they did investigate, it was unlikely they would find anything. The admiral didn't seem to be the caring type when it came to matters like that. He just liked sitting in his comfy chair and pretending he owned the place.

It was apparent he didn't.

We made it to the ship, and the moment the doors shut, Jonathan turned to the two of us.

"You imbéciles!"

"There it is," I whispered.

"You have potentially ruined everything we have worked hard to achieve! If someone finds out, we will be arrested, and there will be no one, I mean no one, who will take our place in hunting Bastien. No one is stupid enough to take this mission, and all the rest are working for him. You understand that, don't you? What you did might have been worse off for Rebecca and Mary."

He sort of had a point there. I didn't really think of it that way. Samuel shook his head. "There is no way anyone could find out. I know how to hide my tracks. And both of us had gloves on, so no fingerprints either."

"But can you be one hundred percent certain of that? Can you look me in the eye and tell me that you know for a fact that someone isn't going to come knocking on that door and arrest us?"

Samuel and I glanced at each other. There was always that possibility, I couldn't deny that.

I turned back to Jonathan. "We know where they went. Once Russ is back, we could go down—"

"And do what exactly? Hack into more computers? If they find out, Bardon will get the report that we went behind his back and he'll have to arrest us. We can't just leave, Nik. Some of us have jobs to go back to."

I frowned. After all this was over, I knew there was no way I was going back into the military— that was for certain. "Fine. We will wait."

"Good. And you two are to stay here. I'll not

have you out mucking everything up even more."

"Okay, whatever," I said as I turned toward the kitchen. "Can you get some takeout then? I would like some Chinese food, if possible."

Jonathan shook his head. "It's clear you and Rebecca had no regard to laws when you were in hiding."

"Yeah, well, we were kind of wanted fugitives. You know—because our military stabbed us in the back."

"That was Sebastien."

"Clearly that is the same thing. All the military side with him. There is no point in doing any of this for the military when it was the military that let him out and able to escape."

"So then what are you on this mission for? Just to save Rebecca?"

I nodded. "Yup. And then I'm getting the hell out of here."

"You know she is wanted too, right?"

"You betcha."

"And if you run off with her, you'll be a wanted fugitive."

"Well, I guess we will have to hide all over again. Pity that."

Jonathan clenched his fist. "Don't put me in that position."

I shook my head. "I'm done talking to you. Go get food or whatever. Samuel and I will be good boys and wait here."

Jonathan clenched his jaw and turned to the door, storming away. I took a seat in the kitchen and let out a breath. Samuel sat across from me.

"Sorry you had to see that," I said. "Just be glad you aren't a part of all this."

"How did it all start? I mean, it seems you and Jonathan are quite close to the mission. Is there any reason?"

I knew I shouldn't be talking to a civilian about it, but at this point, it didn't matter. He knew a lot already, and he could just find out by hacking. "Jonathan, Walrum, and I were all given a mission after graduating from the academy to work under Sebastien and find any evidence of him doing human experiments. That went on for years, and we found no signs. He left no trace of anything he was doing. Then, after a few years, Rebecca became one of our comrades, but she didn't know about our mission—Sebastien simply took her on as a new recruit.

"A few years passed, and we hadn't known it at the time, but Rebecca and Sebastien were an item. It makes sense now. Then something happened and they broke up. After that Rebecca spent more time with us, and well, her and Walrum became an item and eventually got engaged. They were going to leave the military and have a happily-ever-after or whatever. Sebastien found out, and then he set us up to appear as if we had killed a representative.

"I had always thought he had set us up because he found out we were on a mission for Admiral Bardon. It wasn't until all this happened that I found out it was because he was mad that Rebecca had moved on and was going to live her life with Walrum. He used Walrum for experimentation, and it worked. Walrum had been completely brainwashed and does everything Sebastien says. Then I suppose you know the rest."

Samuel raised his eyebrows. "That's quite a

messed-up story."

"It is."

"I can see why you worry about Rebecca's safety. I would too. It makes me worry even more for Mary, to be honest."

"Sebastien is just using her to get to Rebecca. She'll make sure Mary is safe. But I'm not sure how Rebecca can keep that up since she can easily get under Sebastien's skin. Hopefully both of them are safe."

"So tomorrow at 0400 hours?"

I nodded. "Yup. And if anyone asks, I forced you into all these things. I already know I'll be thrown in jail for treason—I don't need you thrown in jail as well. I already have enough burden I carry with me."

He let out a laugh. "Oh, I have done a lot of things in the past. But I'll definitely lie about it all. I don't want to go to prison. Besides, I know you won't get caught. You and Rebecca seem like you could run away from the law as long as the two of you lived."

I chuckled. He wasn't wrong there—I really

believed we could. But first thing was first—I had to find her and get her out of there once and for all.

And make Sebastien pay for the crimes he had committed.

CHAPTER XIII

Rebecca

It was a very fancy restaurant—I gave Sebastien that. There was a private room waiting for us in the back, and there were a lot more officials than I thought possible. Were all of them really his friends? I recognized a few from the time I had spent at Sebastien's side just like this.

I wanted to throw up.

But I kept the smile on my face as I intertwined my arm with his. All the officials had women with them as well, and I prayed that they weren't abused and were there by their own free will. More than likely they were all paid in one form or another. I didn't blame them—these men were rich and could grant any wish that one had. In another life, perhaps I could have done that. It would have probably been a lot less painful.

Bastien pulled out a seat for me, and I smiled and thanked him. I glanced over at everyone. If I wasn't mistaken, all the men here were rulers over this planet and were admirals in the military. I wanted to leave immediately, mainly because I might have caused some messes on this planet when I was on the run with Nik. I didn't know if they knew it was me, per se, but I also didn't want to find out.

"Admiral Wilde, it is a pleasure for you to join us," one man said in Japanese. I believed his name was Admiral Takahashi.

Bastien smiled and replied in the same language. "And it is a pleasure to be here. Thank you for lending out your building. It has been most helpful, isn't that right, *meine Liebchen*." He grabbed my hand and kissed it.

I quickly wiped the look of shock off my face. "Yes, it is most beautiful. I love the decor."

"Leave it to a woman to comment on the decor." He laughed. I thought about smacking that sexist face of his but decided against it.

They kept on talking about mundane things, and I simply nodded, chiming in here or there with comments that were expected of me. Eventually food was brought out and I grabbed the tempura and vegetable sushi, which wasn't technically sushi but always looked the same since it was prepared the same way. I even grabbed some Inari sushi.

Bastien hadn't been lying—there really was some food for me. He was capable of telling the truth from time to time.

I watched as the others ate their sushi covered with fish or fishlike substances. Supposedly all meat and animal products were made in a lab, but there had been many reports of places using actual animals. It was usually rich areas that wanted more *refined* things. I had a feeling what they were eating was the real deal, and it made me sick.

But I couldn't let that show or else Bastien would get mad. I just prayed they wouldn't offer me one as I knew I wouldn't be able to refuse.

I dunked my sushi in some soy sauce and wasabi and took a bite. I added a bit too much wasabi and tried not to cough. Wasabi was always fine for one bite, and then the next it would be utterly spicy.

It had been a while since I had some good Japanese food like this. I especially loved the tempura and ate more than my share. It didn't matter since waitresses brought out even more to fill the empty plates.

After a while, everyone had finished eating and Bastien moved the conversation toward what they were really meeting for.

"So, have you all taken time to think about my proposal?"

Takahashi nodded to the women, and they all got up to leave. I started to stand when Bastien grabbed my wrist.

"Not so fast. You are staying here for the conversation."

I let out a breath as I sat back down. I had hoped I could join them in the other room as I didn't want to be here any longer. I wasn't going to try anything since they were all women who could tattle to their husbands for me. No, I would have just kept quiet. Or talked to them for a bit about other stuff, just out of curiosity.

The women all left, and Bastien began what he wanted to talk about. "You all know that I'm wanted by the Nreff Nation for the experiments that you all helped finance."

They nodded, and I widened my eyes. Seriously? These men financed them? I truly had no respect for officials any longer. It was completely gone.

"And as you learned from the report, we were successful. All the information is in the encrypted messages I had sent you. Now, with this information and with the T.O.W.E.R. treaty coming up, I hope you all will do the right thing and not sign. We had discussed earlier that you would talk to the Regit Republic about getting them to side with you to declare war on the Nreff Nation for these experiments that you all now have evidence of them doing." He smiled. "So where do you all stand in this?"

The men glanced at each other. "Although we do not want to sign the peace treaty, we are not sure we can convince the Regit Republic to side with us. They have been very close to the Nreff Nation for quite some time, and we are afraid that they might side with them if war broke out."

I let out a laugh. "As if the Regit Republic really sides with anyone."

Everyone was quiet as they stared at me. Shit. I needed to learn how to keep my mouth shut.

Bastien smiled. "Oh, do tell?"

"I mean, in my experience of working with them, all they care about is money and power. The Nreff Nation, who is the same way, isn't going to offer them anything they want. What you need to do is make them an offer they just can't refuse. Ships, guns, whatever they need."

I couldn't believe I was helping these guys, but I had already opened my mouth and I would need to finish my thought. And it was true, which wasn't my fault.

Takahashi stroked his beard. "You think so? They have always partnered with the Nreff Nation—more so than they have sided with us on any matters. You think money would make them change their mind."

"I believe so. If not, there are always the Zalia Democracy. They are quiet and keep to themselves, but the quiet ones are usually the ones who have a plan of action if all goes to hell. It would be wise to turn to them as well."

Bastien patted my leg, making me jump a little. "That's my *Liebchen*. Always planning out strategies. That's why we make a great team."

I did not want to be on his team, but I needed to get by so I could survive another day—so I could get Mary out of there.

"The only problem is if they find out you were working with Admiral Wilde here, or if any evidence ever came out that you helped finance his experiments, they might all turn on you. But if you all feel that was kept quiet enough and that you don't have to worry about it, then there is no need to worry."

Those were probably the wrong words, but they were true. The men stirred in their seats.

Bastien glared at me as he smiled. "And as they all know, I cover my tracks. There is no evidence anywhere, here or in Nreff Nation, that my experiments were financed by the YamaXie. In fact, if Admiral Bardon really dug deep, it would appear as if officials in the Nreff Nation had financed it all. The money had gone through quite a few accounts, so we were all safe. Well, except for me. They all know I was behind it."

"Well, isn't that lucky," I commented. "You all are safe and can go on to convince the other nations to turn on the Nreff Nation." Until Bastien goes and convinces another nation to turn on the other. I didn't say that out loud, but I knew it was the truth.

"There will be a meeting with the Regit Republic soon," Admiral Tanaka said. "We will discuss the matters then and get back to you."

Bastien nodded. "That's great to hear. Now, how about some dessert? I heard your mochi here is to die for."

CHAPTER XIV

Nik

It was 0400 hours. I slowly slipped into my clothes and stepped out into the corridor. So far the coast was clear. I pocketed my ID card and headed to where our ship was docked to the patrol.

Samuel showed within a minute, and we both nodded to each other as we began to open the door to the port.

"And where do you think you two are going?"

I let out a breath as I turned to find Jonathan standing there in his pajamas.

"Morning stroll. You know how I can get restless."

"Right." Jonathan nodded at Samuel. "Him too?"

I nodded. "Yup. And Jonathan?"

"What?"

"I'm sorry about this." I pulled out my trank gun and shot him straight in the chest. He went down—hard.

Samuel stared wide-eyed at his sleeping body. I pushed him forward. "Let's get out of here before he wakes up and kills me."

He quickly nodded, and we hurried out of the ship and toward where we could get on a passenger cruiser since there were sometimes a lot of people who didn't have ships and wanted to travel. Cruisers to a good chunk of the main planets were available for passengers. Samuel and I grabbed two tickets to New Tokyo and got on board. Luckily there were quite a few cruisers and they left on the hour. And it took about two hours for the tranks to wear off, so we had plenty of time.

Samuel and I took a seat next to the window and stared out at the stars. This was probably the worst idea I had ever had, but I had to do it. I was used to being a wanted man—not to mention the only thing waiting for Rebecca would be prison if she went back to Nreff Nation. This was the only way for the two of us to be together and survive.

"You think he'll send anyone after us?" Samuel whispered.

I shook my head. "No, I don't. He doesn't know where we are going yet and won't know until he gets that warrant. Hopefully, by then, we will have our answers and he can just clean up the mess."

"And you two used to be best friends?"

I turned back to the stars. "Once upon a time, we were. But now I have a feeling he won't ever want to see my face again."

The ride to New Tokyo took an entire day. There wasn't much to do on the ship other than eat and drink and sleep. We didn't have money for a cabin, so we fell asleep in the chairs that we had. They were at least somewhat comfy, so I got a few hours of sleep.

Once we'd made it to the spaceport, we did the same as we had done at the border and snuck through the vents to grab information off a computer. I jammed the lock, and Samuel skimmed through the information.

"If they didn't lie on the manifest, I think I found the ship. It's still docked here since the owners went planet-side. It all checks out, including the false IDs that they all made. They should be down there on New Tokyo."

"Does it say what city they are staying in?" I asked.

Samuel shook his head. "No, just whether they went to the planet. Once we get to the planet, it's going to be a whole different journey to try to find them."

"But at least of all the planets, we know where to look, so that's a bonus. If I had to guess, however, he's probably being housed by an official of some sort. Can you get a list of all the buildings that are owned by the government and military and download it on your phone?"

Samuel nodded. "Of course. Who do you think I am?"

"One person I'll never piss off."

"You know that's right."

Samuel typed on the keyboard, and soon enough, his phone beeped.

I raised an eyebrow. "That's it?"

"Yup. There are quite a few buildings in the capital alone and around the entire planet. It's going to take us quite a bit of time to find her if we aren't lucky like we have been so far."

He was right—so far we had been quite lucky. I nodded. "Right. Let's get out of here before they notice something is up."

Samuel put everything back to how it was, and we both headed to the vent panel. I helped him up, and right before I joined him, I unjammed the lock and quickly got into the shaft with him.

We were going to find her, I could feel it. We would find some other clue, and we would get her out of there. There was no doubt in my mind.

CHAPTER XV

Rebecca

The walk back to the hotel or whatever we were staying at was the worst.

I could tell Sebastien was angry at what I said—that I might have given those men some doubt about trusting him. It wasn't my fault—he should have let me hang out with the other women.

Taking a few deep breaths, I kept in stride with

him, mainly because he had my arm and was not letting go. He wasn't exactly squeezing it hard, but he was definitely making sure I wasn't going to make a run for it. He didn't need to do that as I wouldn't get far in these heels.

We didn't talk to each other, which was good because I would have said something else to make him mad. I didn't care anymore. He had me locked away in his ivory castle, and he knew as well as I that I wasn't the best of prisoners. I wouldn't fight it for Mary's sake, but I also wouldn't hold my tongue either. He should have known better than to bring me along tonight; he should have let me stay in my room.

As we got to the elevator, Sebastien pushed the button for my floor, which was some relief. As the doors closed, he let out a deep breath.

"What am I going to do with you, Rebecca?"

I shrugged and smiled. "Let me go?"

He stroked my cheek. "You know as well as I that isn't possible."

"Then I have no idea why you are keeping me around. I'm not going to do as you wish. I am not going to become your plaything again."

Bastien lowered his hand and smiled. It wasn't a sadistic smile, which frightened me even more. "You were never my plaything, Rebecca. As I have said time and time again. I love you with all my heart."

I wanted to argue with him, but I knew it was no use. He didn't know what it meant to love—he didn't have a heart. He saw people as objects and used them for his pleasure. There was nothing he could say that would change that fact.

The elevator doors opened, and he walked me to my room. There was a guard stationed in the hallway even though I wasn't there. So Bastien was always making sure I was being watched. That was good to know. From what I could tell, there was only one guard, but that could easily change per his whim.

"You don't have to walk me to my room. I'm sure the guard will make sure I'll get there safely," I commented.

Bastien patted my hand. "Nonsense. Besides, the two of us need to have a little chat."

That was the worst word coming out of his mouth—chat. I took a long breath and let it out slowly, preparing myself for whatever he had in store for me. I had a feeling it wouldn't be anything fun.

We'd made it to my room, and I stepped inside. Bastien closed the door behind us. I sat down on the couch.

"Was there anything you needed? I'm kind of tired and would like to get ready for bed," I commented as he took his jacket off and threw it on one of the other chairs.

"I said we had things to talk about, didn't I?"

He took a seat on the other side of the couch. He wasn't right next to me, but he was still closer than I wanted him. He placed his arm on the top cushion of the couch and leaned his head against it.

"Where did we go wrong, Rebecca? Why are you so quick to lash out?"

I blinked. "You are joking, right? Like, you can't be serious right now."

"I am as serious as I have ever been. What went wrong?"

"Well," I began. "Let me think. You have been experimenting on humans, torturing them, killing people who really shouldn't be killed for decades now to start."

He shrugged. "As you've seen, I was paid to do those things. Many people in multiple governments have given me funding for the things I have done. I was just a means to an end for them, and they are a means to an end for me as well."

"Oh really? And what end is that?" I asked, actually curious. I wanted to know what a madman's reasoning was.

"Power, of course. I have many officials in all the governments wrapped around my finger. Not to mention once this war begins, I'll have a never-ending cash revenue, so I'll be able to buy even a building such as this. I could buy you anything you've ever wanted."

"I want my fiancé back. Can you buy him back?"

"He is still alive—I kept him alive just for you."

I shook my head. "No, you did this to torment me. None of this was for me. You did it to get back at me for moving on."

Bastien clenched his fist. "You weren't supposed to get engaged."

"And you weren't supposed to be sleeping around while we were together."

"I told you countless times now, those women meant nothing to me. I only care about you."

"Then let me be free. Let me get on with my life. If you cared about me, you would have let me go long ago. No, you want me because you think you own me."

He took a moment, as if trying to have some kind of comeback that wouldn't make me slap him. There were no words that could ever make what he did better. And there were no words to convince myself that I wasn't at fault either. I had done all the things he asked of me—killed countless people under his orders. But just because I knew I had done wrong didn't mean I had to spend the rest of my life with him. I didn't have to convince myself that loving him made it all right. I had moved on— I had grown and realized that was not a way to live. I would pay for my sins, and so would he.

"Fine, Rebecca. You want to be free?"

I narrowed my eyes. "Why do I feel like this isn't going to end well?"

He smiled as he stood up. With a swift movement of his hand, he grabbed my hair. He yanked on it and led me to the door.

"If you want freedom so much, then perhaps you should get rid of the only thing keeping you here!" he shouted as he dragged me down the hallway toward the elevator.

"What are you talking about? Let me go!" I screamed.

"Your precious Mary! If she was gone, then you would be free! You could find some way to sneak away, like you always did, and get out of here!"

My eyes widened as we got into the elevator. "Please don't hurt her! I'll be good. I swear!"

"We are far from that now, Rebecca. You had your chance. It's clear you are going to be a thorn in my side the entire way, so we might as well get rid of the reason you've stuck around."

My mind raced, trying to figure out how I was going to get out of this and save Mary. I wouldn't let her die—I wouldn't let him kill her. That was the promise I had made, and I didn't go back on my promises.

He continued to drag me by my hair all the way to her room. Guards we passed stared at me, but they didn't say anything. They knew better than to get involved with Bastien.

Bastien opened the door to where Mary was being kept. The room was similar to mine—a large studio with nice decor. She had been on the couch, watching television, when we interrupted her.

Throwing me on the floor, Bastien tossed me a knife. "Do it, Rebecca. Kill her and you'll be free!"

Mary stood up and backed away. "What's going on?"

"I'm not going to hurt her. Just leave her alone!"

"Why not? You want to be away from me—you don't want to be a part of my life any longer. If you kill her now, I'll let you go. You can go find Nik and live together in some fucked-up ship, or hell, you can go running back to Rolf and fuck him as much as you want like the whore you are!"

I glared up at him. "You realize we both slept with each other to get to you, right? And damn, he is one hell of a ride."

His shoe came straight into my stomach. I curled over, wincing.

"Rebecca!" Mary called from the corner where she hid behind a pillow. As if that were going to help.

"Kill her, Rebecca! Or I will!"

My eyes widened, and I struggled to stand. I grabbed the knife. "I am not going to kill her, and there is no way I'll let you hurt her, you fucking bastard."

He let out a laugh. "Well, that's rich. How many people like her have you killed over the years? How many people pleaded for their life just like she is doing now? What is different about her compared to all the others?"

"Because I have learned I need to put my foot down somewhere. I'm not like all your other men."

He nodded to the knife. "What, are you going to stab me now?"

I was definitely thinking about it, but I knew if I missed, which was more likely than not, he would take it all out on Mary. I threw the knife at his feet.

"Get your kicks elsewhere. I'm tired of playing your games."

He picked up the knife and shook his head. "I thought you were better than this, Rebecca. I guess I was wrong."

With a flash of movement, the knife went straight into my torso. The familiar sting of the blade caught me off guard. I went down to my knees, trying to apply as much pressure to the wound that I could.

Bastien stared down at me and tossed the knife at my side. "Here, if you change your mind. I'll leave you here for a while to get your thoughts straight."

He turned and left me sitting there, bleeding out. My vision became a bit blurry, and I punched my leg to keep myself from passing out.

Damn him. Damn him to hell itself.

CHAPTER XVI

Nik

I stared down at the planet as we made our way to the shuttle. I couldn't believe we were here—the last place we knew Rebecca was at. She might not still be on this planet, I knew that, but I had to keep my hopes up—I had to believe she was still here and was safe and sound.

I knew the last part wasn't going to be true—not

when it was Sebastien who had her. But I was closer, and soon she would be in my arms.

And then the bastard could die.

I hoped Jonathan wasn't too pissed off at me. Odds were that he was. He probably had one hell of a headache after hitting the ground like that, not to mention the tranks caused a pretty massive migraine. I had a feeling Bardon was not ever going to welcome me back with open arms, and I didn't particularly blame him. I would be pretty pissed as well if someone knocked out the love of my life.

But I couldn't wait—I had to get to Rebecca. And besides, Samuel was going to run off on his own if I didn't go with him, and that would have been irresponsible of me. I had to make sure this civilian was fine.

Yeah, no one was going to believe that. I didn't even believe my own words as I said it. Either way, there we were—going after Sebastien on our own. No backup, no real plan…

I fucked up. We really needed to come up with a plan. Perhaps Jonathan was right—I should have stayed behind so we had a more solid plan. But if we waited, Sebastien would be able to get farther away from us and perhaps we would never catch him.

And the treaty meeting was so close now.

I didn't care one way or another how that went. At this point, all the systems were so corrupt that I didn't feel stopping Sebastien would do anything to make them go smoothly. Rebecca and I would be long gone—and we would hide somewhere where war didn't matter and we could just be together.

Was that selfish?

Probably, but after everything we had gone through, I had given up on the government and society. I had a feeling I wasn't the only one.

Samuel was playing on his phone. He was staring at it almost—not blinking—as his thumb went over the touchpad. I wondered if he was searching for something for our mission or checking something else out.

There were a lot of people on this ship—more so than was on a typical transport ship from the planet to the spaceport on any of the Nreff Nation planets.

I had been on a few busy ones in the Regit Republic, but that was only on certain planets. Families were crowded together, and many of the individuals who were traveling kept to themselves. Just like what Samuel and I were doing.

"I think I might know what city they are in," Samuel said as he kept staring at his phone.

My head whipped around. "Really?"

He nodded. "There is an event coming up—one with a lot of officials and such. They will be discussing the peace treaty."

"What makes you think he'll be there? He is wanted, you know."

"In the Nreff Nation, but not here. He may not be present for what is videoed by the news, but there are parts where not even newscasters can attend. I have a feeling he'll be at that part. I don't think it's a coincidence that he escaped and came here when this is going on."

Samuel had a point—he always had plans going on. "When is the event?"

"Day after tomorrow."

I bit at the dead skin on my lip. We had a lead,

but it was still a couple of days away—a couple of days where what we did may catch up to us.

"Can you see if that warrant went through?"

Samuel glanced up at me. "I can try. But not on here. It would have to be on an actual computer."

"We can get one at a hotel."

"Do you have a way to charge that on a card Jonathan can't get traced?"

I frowned. "No, but he'll need a warrant then, wouldn't he?"

Samuel laughed. "Good point. But the bank will give info to the military without a warrant. We will have to borrow some money…"

"I'm not stealing."

He sighed. "Fine then, I guess we will have to move your money around a bunch so they can't pinpoint."

"That sounds fine to me. Can you keep some somewhere for after I get Rebecca and run? We will need a bit of cash starting out."

He nodded. "Sure thing."

"And if anyone asks, I forced you to come with me."

"Oh, don't worry, that was going to be my story either way. No offense."

"None taken. I would use me if I were in your shoes as well."

Samuel began tapping on his phone. I let him do his thing while I thought about what we were going to do. Two days was a long time to wait to save someone, but short to come up with a plan—especially when there were just the two of us.

But good thing he was a hacker. We at least had that on our side.

We found a pretty nice hotel that wouldn't cost an arm and a leg. Samuel did his thing, and we were able to pay for a couple of nights. Samuel requested a computer, and we headed up to our room.

The room had two beds and had a view of the city. There were many skyscrapers in the downtown area. I wondered if Rebecca was in one of them, planning her own way out of the mess she was in.

It was a shame that each window, although clear

to look out of, actually had ads for different business when you peered at them from the other side. I couldn't see into any of the buildings around us. It made sense for privacy but was frustrating when it came to searching for anyone.

Samuel opened up the laptop and began typing away. I had no idea how all that worked. I imagined it took years to be as good as he was showing himself to be.

"How long have you been at this?" I asked.

His eyes didn't leave the computer screen. "Oh, you know, about a decade."

"Have you done anything I should know about?"

He let out a laugh. "Oh, you don't want to know all the things I have done, trust me."

"Touché. I'll pretend I didn't hear that then."

"It's best that you do that. But what I'm doing now isn't exactly good, if there really is a definite good and bad out there. I like to think everything is morally gray, you know?"

I did know that feeling all too well. The things Rebecca and I had to do over the years were far from legal and far from good. We had smuggled drugs and weapons. We never smuggled people though. That was where we drew the line. And perhaps we had taken out a syndicate along the way somewhere because that was what they asked of us.

Which was why Rebecca and I couldn't visit certain planets.

"Here it is," Samuel said as he nodded to the screen. "It appears they did get the warrant earlier this morning."

"So Jonathan is more than likely on his way."

"Yup—probably will get here before the meeting."

"Do you think he'll find us?"

"Not through following the credit, no, but he could if he asked around. It would be a low chance, to say the least."

"What about the meeting? Do you think he'll know to search there?"

Samuel shrugged. "That's a possibility. I'm not sure what Admiral Bardon's plan was."

Great, now they would have to stay clear of Jonathan in the meantime. I knew I should have waited for everything, but that warrant could have been days out.

"Can you keep track of where he is?"

Samuel shrugged. "I can see if he comes to this planet, but past that, there isn't much I can do. This planet is large, and there are a lot of hotels and such."

"Knowing if he is here will be good enough. Keep an alert on that or whatever."

"Will do." He went back to typing.

I turned my attention back outside. I would have to think hard to come up with a plan that would get us to where Mary and Rebecca were, to take out Sebastien, and to do it all without getting caught by Jonathan. Perhaps Jonathan would look the other way.

It wasn't something I was going to count on—not after what I had done. But he left me with no choice, and I prayed he looked at it that way as well.

CHAPTER XVII

Rebecca

Bloody hell, stab wounds hurt.

I grimaced as I applied pressure. From what I could tell, Bastien didn't hit anything vital. He knew where to stab someone so he could leave them to wallow in pain for a while and still be fine. So did I, which was why I wasn't too concerned.

What I was concerned about was the fact Mary

was frantically running around, trying to help me. She had grabbed a towel from the bathroom, and that was what I was currently using to apply pressure. I lifted it and peered at the wound.

Yup, it was still there. And he ruined this perfectly good dress too. I kicked off my shoes and sighed as I lay down on the wood floor. This was completely bullshit. He was like a cranky five-year-old throwing a tantrum when his toys wouldn't behave. I let out a breath. At least I was able to keep Mary safe. For the time being anyway.

I didn't know what to do. My best bet was trying to persuade Walrum to help us, but I didn't know how much I was going to see him. If I requested him, Bastien would know something was up. I just couldn't win.

"I don't know what to do, Rebecca. What do you need?"

I shook my head. "Nothing, just let me sit here in my misery."

"I'm so sorry—this is all my fault. If I hadn't let myself be captured, you would have been able to get away by now."

I shook my head. "No, probably not if we are honest. He's always had me on a short chain. He would have just used some other means to get me to do what he wants."

Mary sat down next to me, hugging her knees. She rocked back and forth. I could tell she had been crying for a while now as I lay there, angry and regretting many decisions I had made throughout my life.

"*Mi dispiace*," she whispered. "For earlier. For saying all this was your fault. I know you were forced to do a lot of things—I can see how scary he is. If I were in your shoes, I probably would have done the same…"

I shook my head. "*Nein*, he wasn't always like that. I can't blame him for all my mistakes. At one time I thought I had loved him. Hell, I know I did. And I did things… Things I don't even want to admit. I could have come forward, but he had been so careful in what he told me that I had really thought I was doing good. But I was blinded by my own feelings. It wasn't until later that I learned the truth and realized what kind of monster he truly was. By then, I was too far into it all, and I never came clean. But if I had, none of this would have happened. Alexandra would be still alive, you wouldn't be in this mess…"

"But you would be in prison."

I nodded. "And that's where I'll be going once this is over—I can guarantee it. That is, if I don't die first." I laughed a little. "I'm not sure which scenario is worse at this point."

Mary didn't say anything but simply stayed next to me. It was strange to have someone worry about me like this. I wasn't used to it. I hardly knew her.

"What about you, Mary? If you could go back and change anything, what would you change?"

She shrugged. "I don't know… I mean, if I could, I would have saved my parents, but Russ and I were too young. For the most part, the two of us have had some good times. I'm sure he is worried sick right about now."

"I bet he is. He is probably helping Nik and Jonathan find us."

"Would they let him, do you think?"

"Do you think permission would stop him from

trying to find his sister?"

She smiled a little. "No, I don't think it would."

"And what about that pilot? Samuel? Are you two still making out?"

Her face turned red. I was glad I was able to get those reactions from her—it distracted her from what was going on currently.

"Yeah, we are going out. He is probably worried sick as well."

"I bet he and Nik are up in arms."

"There's something else…"

My eyes widened. "You're pregnant?"

She shook her head quickly. "No, nothing like that. It's just… Samuel wasn't just a pilot. The military doesn't know this, but he's also a hacker. And really good at it."

I moaned as I sat up. "You're telling me he could hack into computers and find files and all that? As in find where we are now?"

She nodded. "As long as he knows where to search. But if anyone was able to tell which direction we were headed."

I bit my lip. If Nik and Jonathan had happened to

the correct border checkpoint, and they went to the restaurant, they would know what time it was to search. But that was some big ifs.

"What is it?" she asked.

There was no point in hiding it—Bastien already knew. "I left a note for Nik. If they ended up at the right border checkpoint and went to that restaurant we went to, they might know when we had our IDs scanned and can find where we headed."

Her eyes widened. "You mean there is a possibility they know where we are?"

"A very, very small possibility. They would have a one in forty chance of going to the right border checkpoint, and then the rest is counting on Nik and Jonathan's love for Italian food."

"That's why you went there? And what you were telling the cashier?"

Did everyone notice that? I thought I had been smoother than that. "*Ja.* It wasn't anything specific, just was for Nik to know he was on the right track."

She nodded. "But it is something. I believe luck will be on our side."

"And if not..." I lay back down. "I'll just use

brute strength and destroy everyone. But we'll have to find the right moment. And I'm not sure if I can keep you safe the entire time."

"I'm willing to do anything to get out of here. Just say the word."

"Good," I said. "Because it might be sooner rather than later."

Bastien eventually came for me. He had brought Walrum and a couple of other men to carry me out of Mary's room and to what I hoped was someone who would patch me up. I hated doctors and needles and spent most of my time trying to get away from them, but this time I was resigned to my fate.

I needed stitches and for them to clean the wound or else I would be even more screwed.

The men set me down on a table. I frowned as I stared up at the bright lights. This was not going to go well—I could already feel it.

I turned to Bastien. "Are you going to brainwash me like you did my fiancé?"

Bastien moved a piece of my hair out of my face.

"No, I would never do something so vile to you."

I felt a needle go into my arm. I turned to the doctor. "What was that you just gave me?"

"Morphine-B. We give it to all patients who have injuries like these," he explained.

I snapped my attention back to Bastien. "You bastard! You know I can't have that! The doctor said—"

"The doctor said if you had another dose, you wouldn't be able to wean off of it." He smiled. "You'll be stuck with wanting another dose forever."

I shook my head. "Why would you do that? Why would you—" I stopped. I wanted to scream. I wanted to jam the closest sharp object right between his eyes. All that work I had done to get off of it—gone. All because he wanted to mess with me.

My body started to react from the meds, and the sweet sensation began to overtake me. I wanted to smile—I wanted to enjoy it—but I couldn't give him that pleasure. I couldn't let him know how much I wanted it—how much I needed it. It was what got me through seeing him—it was what got me through the nightmares. Taking it was the only time my mind and body were truly at peace.

But I didn't want to be addicted—I didn't want to need it forever. I wanted to stay clean so I could know how to handle my own emotions and deal with my own sins without my body making the decision for me. But now that choice was gone.

"I'll get you for this, Bastien." I turned to him, forcing myself to stay angry. "I'll make you suffer."

He leaned in close, his lips inches from my own. "I would like to see you try, *meine Liebchen*. You are mine to play with, and I'll not let you go this time."

I felt the drowsiness begin to set in. I blinked slow blinks. I turned to Walrum, and in the second I had been conscious, I saw the worry and regret that was on his face.

CHAPTER XVIII

Nik

We decided to check out the building that the event was going to be at.

Pretty much we were casing the joint, and I was a bit hesitant, as Jonathan could be here any moment, or Bardon could have alerted any Nreff Nation authorities where we were and had them sweep the area. If he did that, however, he could put

Jonathan's mission at risk and alert Sebastien we were here. Hopefully caution would be on our side and they would simply let us be.

Things, however, never went that smoothly. So I stayed on alert and looked out for anyone who could be watching us.

The other reason we decided to check out the place was so that Samuel could see what type of systems he would need to hack. We would just have to get him in on the day of, as he didn't have any equipment set up beforehand. There was also the possibility of security sweeping the place before the event started, and if they found the evidence, then they would have been onto us. No, it was better for us to simply prepare everything the day of and find a way in.

"We know there will be waiters and catering," I commented as we stepped inside. "So our best bet is to steal some of their clothes and sneak in that way."

"Odds are, however," Samuel whispered, "they will be scanning all the IDs of the waiters and anyone working that night for security reasons."

"Which is why it's good we have someone who can hack into systems and get us some IDs that will work."

Samuel let out a breath. "I can't magically do everything, you know."

"But can you do that?"

He nodded. "Yeah, I can. It will take me a bit, but I can get it done. We just need to find a manifest. I don't think this building will have it but whoever is putting on the event."

"There should be someone here today going over everything. Perhaps we just need to bump into them and get the data?"

Samuel glanced around. "Problem is there are dozens upon dozens of people in this venue. It will be hard to figure it out, not to mention their data will be protected. I can just scan for it."

"What if we stole it?" I asked.

"Then you would have one great sleight of hand because if someone stole a tablet from my hands, I think I would have noticed."

He had a point there. I tapped my fingers on my crossed arms. We needed to get on that roster, but first we needed to figure out where that roster was. Anyone here could be part of the event, or perhaps no one was here and I had been completely wrong.

"Then first let's see if we can get a map of this place and an idea where everything will be held," I said as I turned to the stairs.

"Right. I have the schematics, but sometimes things change and rooms get rearranged."

The building we were in was part hotel, part dining and event hall. I had a feeling they completely booked the hotel out the night of the event and would be sweeping every floor, which would take some time. More than likely they left it empty tonight so they could begin.

With modern security, it was hard to sneak into places like this—that was why what Samuel did was so impressive, especially since he hadn't been caught. If it weren't for the fact it was illegal, the military would be able to use his skills. They weren't supposed to do anything against the law, other than being able to protect themselves if they were being attacked. However, with the peace treaty maybe not getting re-signed, it was possible that they would need hackers.

"So far these schematics are correct. I think we can go off them. Security will be on high alert. I think you are right—the only way to get in is if we are on the roster. More than likely they will bring in their own cooks and waiters, to be safe. We will need to find someone with that list."

"And we can act as if we are with the event party. If we ask questions, they might alert the real planners and they will move the event to somewhere else."

Samuel let out a breath. "Yeah, unfortunately that is the case. Keep your eyes and ears open for anyone you think could be involved."

I nodded. "Let's split up and see if we can find anything on our own. Meet back at the entrance in an hour?"

"Sounds good to me."

I started wandering around, searching for anything that appeared out of the ordinary. I listened carefully to different conversations, but many were speaking in languages I didn't understand. Some were in English and German but not many. I more than likely wouldn't be able to understand those who were planning the event, so I had to watch people's actions more than anything.

There were quite a lot of people holding tablets, which wasn't helpful. There were a lot of businessmen and women meeting up and talking about God knew what. I watched to see if any of them were talking to the workers of the hotel, but none of them were.

Perhaps we were going about this wrong—perhaps we needed to come up with another plan. The problem was, I had no idea what else to do.

This was where Jonathan and Bardon came in handy—they were good at missions.

As I glanced down at the entrance area of the hotel, I saw a familiar face. It was Sebastien Wilde.

I hid behind a pillar as I peeked down. I couldn't let him see me—I couldn't let him know I was here.

First thing was first, what should I do about this? Should I hide until he was no longer here? Should I see what he was up to?

Or should I follow him and let him lead me to

Rebecca? That would be a risky move, but what if it was our only chance? What if he didn't come to the event, or we didn't get into the event, and this was the only chance to find her?

I didn't waste time on contemplating—I snuck down the stairs. I was careful to make sure he didn't see me as I hung around the back of the entry. He was talking to someone—more than likely part of the event or a government.

So it was true—people in most governments didn't care about what he did and wanted chaos and destruction. How could people be so driven by power and wealth to not care about its people? It would be the first war in centuries—an intergalactic war that could kill millions.

It all left a nasty taste in my mouth. It was all beyond me, and I doubt I could have done anything to stop something that was in motion, but at least I could stop him from benefiting from it all.

After a while, Sebastien stopped talking to the man and went back outside. I counted to five and headed outside myself. Luckily there were a lot of people around, so I wouldn't seem too out of place.

It took me a few moments, but I was able to spot Sebastien. He was heading down the street by himself. I thought about shooting him right then and there, but I needed to know where he was keeping Rebecca. If I killed him now, it was possible she would be killed on the spot.

I couldn't guarantee that the building he was heading toward was where Rebecca was, but I knew it was at least a good chance, as I doubted he had many other errands to run.

He walked for a few blocks, and I kept my distance. I was surprised he didn't have anyone with him, as he was a wanted man after all. Did he really have that much confidence in himself that he thought he could stop anyone? And that he had everyone wrapped around his finger that they wouldn't hurt him?

Perhaps he did. I couldn't kill him because I needed to find Rebecca, and others didn't want to kill him because they wanted power. Or perhaps he had other things in place to make sure no one betrayed him.

He stopped in front of a large skyscraper and

entered it. I stared up at it. This was where he was staying. It was likely Rebecca was in there. It was a large building, so, it was going to be a real pain to find her.

But at least I knew where she probably was now.

I headed back to where Samuel would be waiting for me. Now we didn't have to pull a whole operation like out of a movie—now we could just sneak into the building where they were being held during the event when he was away.

We had lucked out.

CHAPTER XIX

Rebecca

It was raining. I was standing in the park, staring up at the clouds. Raindrops hit my face. It felt refreshing—as if it could wash away everything I had ever done.

Next to me was Walrum. He was smiling at me as he watched me enjoy the storm we were in the middle of.

"You are so strange, Rebecca," he said with a smile.

I wrapped my arms around him and kissed him. "But you love me for it, don't you?"

"*Jawohl*. From now to eternity."

My eyes blinked open. It was a dream—a dream about a memory that I had with Walrum. I hadn't had dreams about him in quite some time. I felt a tear escape my eye, and I wiped it away.

Memories of everything that had happened before I passed out came back to me. Bastien had stabbed me, then he left me to be in pain and then used morphine-B on me. It would be nearly impossible for me to get off of it, or at least it would take some time.

But that was the least of my worries.

I had to focus now. I had to find a way out of here.

"Have a nightmare or something?"

I jumped up and grimaced as the stab wound was still fresh. Walrum was sitting on the couch. I guess waiting for me. I was back in my room, much to my surprise. I expected to wake up on the operating table with my worst nightmare standing above me.

"Be careful," Walrum said as he got up. "You wouldn't want to reopen that wound of yours."

I stared at him, confused as to what he was up to. "Why are you here?"

He shrugged. "I was ordered to make sure you woke up and were fine."

"Or at least as fine as I can be, right?" I smiled a little. "So I guess you completed your mission and are free to go now."

Walrum glanced at the door but didn't budge. It was as if he was contemplating something. I glanced down and found that I was still in my dress. Well, at least they didn't change my clothes without my permission. That was one good thing about non-legit medical places—they didn't always take off clothes. I always hated it when they did that anywhere official.

"I don't think this is fair."

I turned to Walrum. Had he really said that? So I had gotten through to him. "What isn't fair?"

"That he used that drug on you, knowing your body was addicted. He did it to mess with you."

I shrugged. "Well, believe me when I say it isn't the worst thing he has done. I'll find a doctor to help me—there are definitely better doctors throughout the systems than on the Nreff military base."

He didn't say anything again but kept glancing around.

Deciding not to care whether he was there or not, I got up to go change. As I moved, I grimaced.

"Let me help you," Walrum said as he reached for me. I stared at his hands, not sure if this was some kind of trick or if I had really gotten through to him.

I took his hands, and he helped me up. "Thanks, I guess."

"Need any help changing?" He gave me a slight wink.

I rolled my eyes. "Are you sure you don't have your memories back? You are starting to sound like the old Walrum."

He smiled a little. "No, I still don't."

Walrum said that with a bit of regret. So that was what was bothering him—he did want those memories back. I debated if I should try to wedge that doubt a little more, if I should let him do it himself. The problem was, as he was acting like this, I was seeing the old Walrum—the man that I had once loved. I cared about him more than anything, and I didn't want to see such sadness in his eyes.

But it wasn't him. This was some experiment of Bastien's. I couldn't let my past affect how I was going to get out of here.

I pushed back the pain and smiled. "You know, once upon a time we came to this planet together for a mission."

He hesitated for a moment, then asked. "Is that so?"

I nodded. "Yup. It was rare to get missions outside the Nreff Nation, but this one had been authorized by the higher-ups. We had to help some agents in the YamaXie find a fugitive. It was a cut-and-dry mission, but you had a lot of problems trying to understand the signs and what everyone was saying. You were out of the loop, but it ended well."

"Now I can speak many languages, so that wouldn't be a problem."

"So you can. That would have come in handy once upon a time."

He fidgeted with his hands. "What about you? Do you speak many languages?"

"A good chunk. Around eight."

"That's a lot. And you didn't have to have them programmed into you."

I shrugged. "Not in the sense you are saying, no. But it took a lot of studying and training. And if I'm not careful, I start to forget words and grammar."

"That makes sense."

We stood there, quiet. He really didn't want to leave. This was strange. It was clear these weren't orders from Bastien, as he wouldn't want him near me like this. He wasn't acting himself, and Walrum remembering everything would be the last thing Bastien wanted.

I turned to my closet. "Well, I'm going to change. You can stay here if you wish. I have no idea what Bastien ordered of you, and it's not like

I'm calling the shots."

I grabbed a black tank and some gray sweats. I was glad I had those options as I definitely didn't want to stay dressed-up fancy. I changed in the bathroom after a quick shower and felt almost as good as new, other than the wound. That would heal up in no time, and I didn't mind it too much since I was used to stab wounds and the like. I was convinced most of my nerves were shot—or perhaps the morphine-B was still in effect.

Stepping out of the bathroom, I found that Walrum was still there. I hated using him like this, but it was the only chance I had. He stood up when he saw me. I glanced around.

"Does this place have a gym or something? I mean, I know I'm a prisoner and all, but I would like to train a bit, just to keep myself in shape. Unless Sebastien won't let me do that either?"

He glanced at the door. "I am not sure. I can ask him. I wouldn't today though, since you have that wound. You need to give it time to heal."

Right, the wounds. Damn. "Oh right. Yeah, I suppose that is a good idea. I'm sure a little bit of training won't hurt it if I'm careful. I guess I can just stretch in here."

I went to the middle of the living area where the rug was and began to stretch my arms. Walrum stood in the middle, confused like a puppy dog. It made me smile a little, as he appeared almost human now.

"Either leave or join me, just don't stand there like a confused idiot."

"Right, sorry."

He joined me in stretching instead of leaving, which was a sign he really was trying to sort all this out. His training had been to do what was ordered of him without question, but now I put doubt in his mind. It was easy—I used the same words that would have sent me spiraling years ago.

We did some simple stretches and then some balancing stretches. It reminded me of all the times the two of us had trained together. We used to mess with each other to make the person off-balance. Without much thought, I pushed Walrum as he was standing on one leg.

He lost his balance and put the other foot down.

"Hey, what was that for?"

I smiled. "We used to do it all the time. It helps with fighting. It's not as if someone you fight will let you take your time to get balanced."

Walrum smiled. "Well, if you want to play it that way."

We played around for a while, trying to get the other person off-balance. We laughed, and for a moment I had forgotten everything—for a moment I thought I was with my fiancé, having a good time.

I shoved Walrum, and he started to fall back but not without grabbing my arm and taking me down with him. He hit the ground with a thud, and I added to the momentum.

"Are you okay?" I asked as I moved hair out of his face. I didn't get off him though. I didn't want to.

He nodded. "Yeah, just got the wind knocked out of me." He laughed. "I don't think I have ever had this much fun before."

I didn't reply to that as I didn't know what to say. He was being kept as a weapon—an experiment. I slowly played with his hair—the hair that I missed.

Walrum moved his hand to behind my head as his eyes lingered on my own eyes and then moved down to my lips. He pulled me in closer and kissed me on the lips.

I didn't know how to feel. I didn't know if I should move away or stay like this for as long as I could as I didn't know if I could ever get a kiss from the man I loved—the man I was supposed to marry. Again.

After a few moments, he turned his head. "What am I doing? I can't be doing this. I don't... I'm not..."

I moved off him and let him rush to the door. He left me sitting there, on the floor, not sure what I should be feeling.

But I knew it was for the better—I knew this doubt could come in handy when I found a way to get out of there.

CHAPTER XX

Nik

"There you are. I was beginning to worry."

I checked the time on my phone and found I was fifteen minutes late. "Sorry, I saw Sebastien and followed him."

His eyes widened. "You did? Where did he go?"

I nodded toward our hotel. "Let's go somewhere where we don't have to worry about anyone hearing us talking."

The two of us headed back to our hotel. Once we were inside, Samuel turned to me.

"Okay, now spill. What did you find out?"

"Sebastien headed down the street and went to that building." I pointed out the window. "My guess is that Mary and Rebecca are there."

"So our plan has changed, hasn't it? That works out—I wasn't able to find any info on the roster for tomorrow."

I took in a deep breath and let it out slowly. "We can go in while Sebastien is at the event—I assume he'll be there, and then we can go and extract the two of them. After that, we can figure out a way to take Sebastien down. Or, hell, we can just let Jonathan take care of that."

"I'm taking care of what now?"

I reached for my gun as Jonathan stepped out of the bathroom and had a gun pointed at me.

"*Scheiße*," I said as I stepped back.

"Yeah, shit is right. You have any idea how much trouble you are in? You are lucky you didn't get caught by the border patrol, but Jacques isn't very happy with the two of you. Especially you, Nik. You know better."

I shook my head. "I don't care what happens to me—I want to get Rebecca out of there."

"And so do I."

"But you want to throw her in jail," I stated.

Jonathan rubbed his face. "I don't *want* to throw her in jail, but all that has come out about her involvement… It's not up to me or Jacques anymore. The people know the truth, and they want her to pay."

I shook my head. "I'm not letting you take her in —after everything she has been through, she deserves better."

"Are you really that closed by love not to see the truth?"

"No, I just know people change, and I know the two of us have done awful things as well while serving him. None of us are innocent. Besides, if we had found evidence earlier, like we should have, she would never have been dragged into this."

"So you feel guilty? That's rich."

"We had a mission, and if we worked faster, then

we would have been able to take him down.”

“You mean if we hadn’t gone by the book, we would have caught him.”

“Exactly.”

“Which is why now you’ve thrown every rule out the window, trying to get to Rebecca. Because you think it will make up for decades of her being involved in this.”

I shook my head. “I just want her safe, that’s all.”

Jonathan and I stared at each other for a long moment when Samuel coughed.

“Look, I don’t want to get in the middle of whatever this is, but let’s be honest—Admiral Wilde doesn’t play by the book. But he’ll be at the event tonight where you, Jonathan, can capture him and take him in. Meanwhile the two of us can go and get Rebecca and Mary and be on our way. Everyone wins. You catch the horrible criminal and can do whatever you want with him, and we will have the people we care about safe.”

“You are a civilian and shouldn’t be in the middle of this.”

Samuel shrugged. “Well, it’s a little late for that

anyway."

Jonathan shook his head. "I'm not supposed to look the other way—what you two did was wrong."

"But do you really want to turn all your attention on us when you need to catch Sebastien?" I asked. "Because we can guarantee we will not be cooperative captives."

Jonathan sighed. "That's true. You two have been a pain in my butt for a while now." He paused, as if contemplating this mess. He put his gun away. "Fine, but we are doing things *my* way, do you understand? All you two will be doing is getting Mary and Rebecca out, do you hear me? Then you come straight back to the base. You do not run off —you do not take things into your own hands— you listen to every command I give."

Samuel and I glanced at each other and shrugged. I turned back to him. "Fine. But let me talk to Bardon about Rebecca. I'm sure he and I will be able to work something out."

Jonathan laughed. "You can try, but as I said before, he is pretty pissed at you."

Right. There was that. "I'll take my chances with

him. Now, I presume Russ is back at your base of sorts."

He nodded. "He is. It's actually also in this hotel. Don't worry, I got two adjacent rooms so that the five of us can stay together. Now come on, let's go fill him in."

Samuel and I followed Jonathan out of the room.

"How did you find us?" Samuel asked. "We were careful to cover our bases."

Jonathan patted his back. "Like I would tell you so you can cover your tracks even better."

I chuckled as we made our way down the halls and up the elevator a ways. Soon we came upon the door, and Jonathan opened it.

Russ was lying on his bed, watching TV. He almost appeared like a teenager when I realized he practically was still one and that I was almost old enough to be his dad. I did not need that realization. Jonathan closed the door behind us as Russ stood up.

"You found them! Took you long enough," Russ commented as he yawned.

"I told you I would have to wait until they got

back to their room. I wasn't sure how long that would be."

Russ turned to us and put his hands on his hips. "How dare you two run off like that."

I raised an eyebrow. Was this kid really going to try to scold me? I was almost twice as old as him.

He went on. "And you didn't even think I wanted to tag along? You were going to go save my *sorella* without me."

Jonathan smacked him on the back of the head. "Then you would also be in trouble, you idiot."

Samuel patted him. "We needed things to run smoothly, and that wasn't going to happen if you tagged along."

Russ stuck his tongue out at him. I rolled my eyes as I sat down on the couch. The two of them were good at what they did, but they were still young. I didn't know if I should be impressed or mortified.

"Remember when we were like that?" Jonathan commented as he sat down across from me.

I shook my head. "No, I was always mature. I never stuck my tongue out at any of you."

Jonathan laughed. "Right. I'm sure I have a picture somewhere…"

"I was joking. Of course I remember all the trouble we got in."

The two of us sat there, quiet, as the other two bickered. I smiled a little at them, but I could feel the pain in my chest from what I had done to Jonathan—one of my best friends. I had betrayed him and his trust and didn't deserve this second chance he was giving me.

"Look, Jonathan, I'm sorry…"

He shook his head. "No, it's fine. I get it. I just wish you would think a little before you act rash. But you and Rebecca became really close when you were in hiding. I can't imagine what you are going through right now. Just… don't go off on your own again, all right? If we work together, we'll be able to pull this off."

I nodded. "Right. I think we can too."

"But first you need to talk to Admiral Bardon."

"Yeah, do you have a video chat set up anywhere I can use?"

"Or, better yet, you can talk to me in person."

My heart felt as if it had skipped a beat. I turned to find Bardon with his arms crossed in front of him. He was frowning as he glared at me.

I smiled innocently. "Admiral, it's good to see you. How have you been?"

CHAPTER XXI

Rebecca

After Walrum left, I was alone in my room for a few hours. I continued to stretch and watch whatever was on the television. Apparently there was a big event nearby tomorrow, and I prayed to God that I wouldn't be dragged to such an event. I had a feeling I would be—it was the type of even that Sebastien used to frequent all the time, mainly because the dignitaries here didn't let any press in, so Sebastien had free rein to attend without being seen.

"Please don't force me to go. Please don't force me to go."

I didn't feel like going anywhere with Bastien again, mainly because I knew I wouldn't keep my mouth shut and then get in some trouble again. It's not like I could stir much trouble anyway, as these people were on Bastien's side. Ugh, this was not fair.

I played the scenario back at the trial over and over again in my head. There were ways for me to have freed Mary. I should have done them, then I wouldn't have been in this mess. I could have run off by now. I was used to running and hiding—there was no way he would have found me this time.

That probably wasn't true, but I could have tried. It would have been better than just sitting here.

But at least I was beginning my plan for getting Mary out of here. Walrum was having doubts, and although I felt bad for using him, it was the only way. Even if it hurt my heart.

Was it possible for him to get his memories back? Alexandra had dedicated her life to studying the brain, but she didn't know how to fix Walrum. That was mainly because he was "remembering" things, although it was all fake. Had she actually had to work with him, she might have been able to do something.

There were hundreds of thousands of people across the systems that he could go to, however. Perhaps a few of them would know how to help him. Did I risk trying to get him out of here too? Or was what he was doing all a part of Bastien's plan?

But he had been my fiancé. Shouldn't I try to help him?

He could also cost Mary her life if this was all some ploy to make me mess up—to test me as Bastien always liked to do. That look on his face seemed genuine enough, however.

But it also seemed genuine when he was in the hospital and I had to go along with his lies.

Walrum had always seemed to be executing Bastien's plans one way or another, whether it was to torment me or not. I couldn't put it past him to do this, so I knew I couldn't risk it.

I pushed back all the memories we had together and tried to keep moving forward. I needed to get Mary out of here, and then I could come back and deal with Sebastien. Then perhaps I could help Walrum. But he wouldn't be my priority.

And then what? What did I do about Nik? If Walrum remembered our life together, did I abandon Nik? Did I live the rest of my life with Walrum?

I rubbed my face. This wasn't the time to worry about this—I needed to focus on the task at hand. I had to get out of here and get Mary a safe distance from Bastien. Then the rest I could worry about later.

As I finished up the last stretch, the door slid open. My heart skipped a beat, thinking perhaps Walrum came back, but it was Bastien. I frowned.

He raised an eyebrow. "And who were you expecting?"

Scheiße. "I thought perhaps Nik found me and had come to save me at last."

Bastien laughed as he made his way to where I was sitting. "And how did you know that he was on the planet?"

My eyes widened. "He's here?"

"Oh, so you didn't know? Then you were expecting someone else."

He got me there. "I had asked Walrum if I could see Mary. I thought maybe it was him coming back."

"Well he never came to me about that, so I doubt you'll see her anytime soon."

"So why are you here? To taunt me with Nik's presence?"

I was glad he had gotten my clue and was right on our tail, but I did not like the fact that Bastien knew he was here. He was going to set him up for a trap.

"That, and to let you know we will be going out tomorrow."

I blew my bangs out of my face. "Damn, are you making me go to that event?"

"Indeed. Do you know why?"

I frowned. "Because you let Nik see where I was

and now he's going to try to break in here while I'm with you at the event."

"Precisely, *meine Liebchen*. And Walrum will be here waiting for him. Isn't that just the greatest plan yet?" He smiled, almost giddy. "My hope is he can capture him so I can make you watch as I end his life, but alas we shall see."

I shook my head. "You're a monster. You know that right?"

He grabbed my chin and forced me to stare at him. "And you make me like this. I wouldn't have to do all this if you just behaved."

"I've done everything you've asked so far. What more do you want from me?"

"If you had been well-behaved, Nik wouldn't know where you were. You are the one that left that little clue for him. I presume he got it if he is this close behind us. So it's your fault I'll have to dispose of him so quickly. If you hadn't done that, they might have never caught up to us, and he would be safe."

I glared at him. I knew he had a point, but I couldn't let myself fall victim to his words. I had to keep on pushing forward.

Besides, Nik could take care of himself. He was skilled in fighting and would know to be on alert. I didn't know if it was just him or if Jonathan was there too. He should be, as Bardon would have sent them both on a mission.

Jonathan would come up with a good plan. He always did.

"So what do you want me to do exactly? Be your arm candy?" I asked as I went through all the scenarios in my head. If Jonathan and Nik knew about the event, they would split their resources—one would be at the event, and the other would try to extract us, although I wouldn't be here for that. Whether Mary would be was another story. If Bastien's goal was to get Nik, he might not care if they try to take Mary. If Nik succeeded, Mary would be out of Bastien's grasp and I could then kill Bastien.

This would go according to plan. It had to.

He released my jaw. "Of course—I wouldn't have it any other way."

"Well, good thing I have the other dresses since

you ruined the one I was wearing."

Bastien shrugged. "I wouldn't want you appearing in the same dress anyway. It would look as if I'm not treating you right."

I gave him a look, then shook my head. "Whatever." Then I remembered what I had asked Walrum. "Oh, can I train a little? I don't want to be out of shape as I haven't exercised in a while."

He laughed. "Do you think I'm a fool?"

"I think you have men with guns who could have them ready the entire time I get a little cardio in."

Bastien pondered that for a moment. "Fine. But not until tomorrow. You need to heal a bit." He held up his finger. "Oh, by the way, since it is getting to be that time." He nodded toward one of the dressers. "Your morphine tinctures are in there. Just make sure not to take too many, all right? They do cost a pretty penny."

I glared at him. "I'll keep that in mind."

He leaned back in the chair. "Whenever you feel you are ready, go ahead. I have all day."

He wanted to watch me suffer—he wanted to see me fall to my darkest state again. I couldn't let him see me like I had been.

But I couldn't exactly go against what my body craved—not when it was playing with my mind. While I may still give in to the drug that he had, that didn't mean I would let him see me at my darkest. I was no longer afraid of him like I had been. I could take this drug, and it wouldn't be the same as it had been. I wouldn't let him get to me.

I stood up, not letting him see the fear in my face —not letting him see how it would cause me to be addicted—how I knew I had no choice. I didn't let him see the fear of knowing he was doing this to control me, and perhaps it would be possible— perhaps I would succumb to his whim for another dose, but I was currently far from that. I wouldn't let it get that far. I couldn't.

Stepping over to the drawer, I opened it to find a few bottles of the drug. I grabbed a small tincture and broke the top and chugged it back. It tasted bitter, but I was used to the taste. Turning back to him, I smiled. "There, are you happy?"

He stood up and made his way over to me. Bastien kissed my cheek, and I didn't move away

—I knew there was no use.

"Not quite. But we are getting there. I'll see you tomorrow, and I'll let Walrum know he can take you to the gym tomorrow, as long as you promise to be a good girl and take your medicine." He stood there, waiting. "Well, do you promise?"

"Sure. *Was auch immer*," I answered. I really wanted to get out of this room, and I knew eventually my body would profess its need for the drug.

"That's *meine Liebchen*."

With that he left me standing there. He closed the door behind him, and once I knew he was out of my hair, I collapsed to the ground, tears running down my face.

"Damn him," I whispered to myself. "Damn him to hell itself."

CHAPTER XXII

Nik

"How have I been, you ask?" Admiral Bardon said with a sigh. "I have been cleaning up your mess is how I have been."

I nodded slowly. "Yeah, I guess you would be…"

He pinched the bridge of his nose. "You know how much trouble you would have been in if they'd caught you? How much trouble I would have been in?"

I bowed down. "I'm sorry, sir. I truly am. I betrayed your trust in me, and I could have blown it all. The problem is that I just"—I shook my head—"I can't imagine what she is going through, and I just want her to be safe. I saw my chance, and I took it. I should have thought about it better and consulted with you."

"The problem, Nik, is I don't know if you're going to disobey me again. I don't know if you'll see a chance that you think is fine and take it and jeopardize the mission. You do realize that, don't you?"

I nodded. "Yes, sir."

Bardon let out a breath. "But I do not have many men at my disposal, so I can't exactly tell you to be off this mission. You just have to promise me you won't do something so reckless again, okay?"

"Yes, sir."

"Now, tell me what you know."

I went on to explain everything we knew. "There is an event tomorrow that we believe Sebastien will be attending. I saw him and followed him to where

I think he is holding Rebecca and Mary. If you'll let us, Samuel and I can try to extract Mary and Rebecca while you and Jonathan go after Sebastien."

"What about me?" Russ chimed in.

I shrugged. "I have no idea—that's up to Bardon."

Bardon answered. "Let me give this some thought. We have found Samuel is quite the hacker, and I'm not sure where he would be the most beneficial. If Sebastien has men watching cameras in the building Rebecca and Mary are in, it might be better that he goes with you. As for you, Russ, you are good with electrical things as well, correct?"

Russ grinned. "One of the best!"

Bardon rubbed his chin. "Is that right? Well then, I might need you with us instead, if that is all right. I might need some mechanics to go off. Nothing dangerous but enough to provide for a distraction."

Russ fidgeted. I had a feeling he wanted to go with us to find his sister, but he was better than I was and knew how to listen to orders.

"Okay. I can do that. What do you need from me?"

"I need you to make some smoke bombs. Can you do that?"

He laughed. "I used to make those all the time in grade school."

I commented, "So like a year ago?"

He frowned. "That's not funny."

Jonathan laughed. "Yes it is. You are practically a child to us. But you are smart, and we don't assume anything because of your age, all right? It's good to be young, believe us. You'll hit an age where you begin to realize, well, you'll see, I guess. Aging is a curse."

Bardon sighed. "You all make me feel so old. Why do you do this to me?"

Jonathan gave him a kiss on his cheek. "I like your gray hairs. It makes you appear even more wise."

"I didn't say anything about my hair being gray. You are actually making me feel even older. Thanks."

"You are most welcome." Jonathan gave him

another kiss. "Now, shall we go and get supplies? Russ, what all do you need? And Samuel, make a list."

Samuel cracked his knuckles. "Oh, do I have a list."

I stood out on the balcony, peering down at the street. Bardon had gotten a bit bigger of a suite than I had that included a balcony. The air was cold, and the wind whipped around the city streets.

Rebecca was out there, more than likely suffering at Sebastien's hand. It would be less than twenty-four hours until I saw her and saved her from all this. I wondered if Bardon had never put us on the mission of getting intel against Sebastien, if he would have still taken her on and caused her all this grief. He had known from the beginning what we were doing and sent us on a giant wild-goose chase. He let her see everything he had done.

And then he tortured Walrum. I had always thought it was because he had found out the truth, but it was because he wanted to punish Rebecca for loving someone else. It made me sick.

"Staring angstily out at the city like some kind of antihero?" I heard Jonathan say behind me.

I turned to him. "Oh, you know me—I have this scar over my eye and all that. I might as well play the part."

He laughed as he joined me, peering down at the city. Anyone afraid of heights would not be stepping out here.

"I'm just going through everything in my mind. I wonder if we will be successful or not."

He patted my back. "We will be—we have to be. This is probably our only shot. If he gets away, we are screwed."

He could say that again. "I think as long as we can get them out of there, it would be better—we won't have to worry about hostages."

"There's that. Although I think Mary is the only one we really have to worry about. Once she is out of his hands, Rebecca will try to take care of the rest. The only reason she hasn't made a move is because of her."

I nodded. That was probably a fact. Rebecca

didn't want anyone else to die because of her. I could understand that feeling.

"What do you think about Sebastien being at the event though? It's going to be heavily guarded, and if it comes out that he was there, it could be a large incident."

"That's their problem, not ours. They are the ones harboring a fugitive."

I shook my head. "Why would they even let him go to such an event? And risk getting caught?"

"They can claim ignorance—that he had lied about everything. Although we have the technology to communicate between systems, there is so much information being transmitted between planets and such they can say they never read it and it all will slide under the rug."

"I don't know about you, but the more I have learned about the military and politics, the more I don't want to serve or belong to any nation."

"What, do you just want to live out of your ship and hope that no one asks questions?"

"Precisely."

Jonathan laughed. "Well, it's not all bad being in

the military. We have made a lot of memories together—ones that I'll always cherish."

I nodded. "As do I. I wished it didn't have to be this way—I wish we were able to go on being best friends—all three of us. All four of us."

Jonathan and I stood quietly as we watched the city below. I watched as people rushed to whatever important thing they needed to go to. Some of them walked as if they were enjoying life, and some appeared as late as ever. I wondered what it would have been like to be a normal citizen—what it would have been like to live my life blinded to what was going on behind the scenes. Would I have been a better person? Would I have had a better life? Would I have found someone to love?

Jonathan patted my back again. "If you need me, I'll be inside, eating dinner. I think they got some pad Thai takeout. It's getting cold, just saying."

"Yeah, I'll be right in. Just give me a second."

Jonathan left me standing there. I took in a deep breath of the city air. It would be over before I knew it, then I could get on with my life. We all could.

CHAPTER XXIII

Rebecca

Today was the big day. Yippee.

I punched the bag that hung before me. Bastien kept his word and had sent Walrum to take me to a gym in the building. There were six men, plus Walrum, holding guns at me as I worked out. No pressure or anything.

Walrum didn't look at me almost the entire time I

worked out. That was fine with me as I didn't want to face him either. I still didn't know how I felt about everything even if I did need to use him to get Mary out of here. I couldn't let on there was anything going on, however, as the guards might report it to Bastien, so I kept my distance.

I didn't exercise too much as I didn't want to reopen my wound. I paced myself, as it wasn't the first time I had worked out with a wound before, and it certainly wouldn't be the last. I knew what to look out for even if my senses were a little dull after taking another dose of the morphine-B.

Punching the bag a little harder, I thought about Bastien. How dare he do this to me, just to get under my skin. I didn't want to be addicted any longer—I didn't want to be suffering—but alas, he was a prick and did it anyway. This wasn't going to be easy to defeat—not after what the doctor had said. I knew there would be a way, but it would take some time.

And time was not something I had.

I supposed in the end it didn't matter because I was either going to die while trying and hopefully succeeding to kill Bastien, or I was going to be arrested and would have plenty of time to go through all the withdrawal symptoms in prison. That would a blast to look forward to.

And then if I did escape and just stayed on the run, well, then I would have to find some sketchy doctor to help me. Great.

I let out a breath as I threw one last punch. That was probably as much as my body was going to handle for the day, as I didn't want to deal with opening the wound. I turned to Walrum.

"I am done. Can we head back?"

He nodded, still not looking me in the eye. The other men lowered their guns a tad as he led me back to the room. A couple of them followed, making sure I wasn't going to pull anything. I wasn't. Not yet anyway.

Walrum walked me all the way back to my room and was about to leave when I stopped him.

"Wait, I had a question and needed some help with something. Come inside."

Walrum eyed me, the first time I saw his dark bluish-green eyes today. "What is it?"

"I just… I want you to help me pick something out for tonight. Bastien can be picky, and I don't want to make him mad. Not again."

He let out a breath. "Fine. I'll see what I can do. I don't know if me picking anything out would help."

That didn't matter, because it wasn't what I really needed him for. He stepped inside and I went to my closet.

"I have a few options. This red one, a purple one, but I don't like purple, and this blue one." I held them all up.

"Well, what is his favorite color? Do you know?"

I made a disgusted sound. "Ugh. Purple."

"Is that why you don't like purple?"

I nodded. "You are quick to pick up on that."

He stepped forward, taking a closer look at the clothes. "Personally, I think you look good in blue. But I suppose you aren't dressing up for me, now are you?"

My heart rate began to quicken. Walrum used to say that to me all the time when we were together —he thought I was beautiful in blue.

"I guess not. But I do like blue. But I should probably wear the color Bastien likes then. God, I hate dresses."

"But you look so beautiful in them."

I laughed. "Perhaps, but they aren't easy to fight in—especially with heels. But I can get away with flats since I'll be wearing the dress he likes the most."

I put them away and let out a sigh. "Thanks for your help."

"You are welcome, but I don't think I really did anything. You already know what he likes and dislikes. You could have easily figured it out."

I hesitated. "Maybe I just wanted your company."

Walrum shook his head. "I can't be doing this. Not now—not when everything is at stake."

"What do you mean everything? Because you have orders from Bastien?"

"Yes. I have to stay here and guard Mary while you and Admiral Wilde go to the event."

I bit my lip. I knew the plan. This was my chance. "So you can capture or kill Nik, right?"

He nodded. "Yes."

I shook my head. "It's all my fault. He's going to be killed because of what I did."

"You shouldn't have gone against the admiral's orders. You knew that."

I wished I could cry on command. It would have come in handy. I peered up, as if I were trying to hold back tears. "He used to be your best friend, you know. You two were inseparable. How ironic it would be if you killed him."

He glanced away. "You know I don't remember that. I have no memory of him."

"I know. It's a shame, really. Most people would give an arm and a leg to have a friendship like the two of you had. And then now…" I let out an ironic laugh. "This is where we are at."

He was silent for a moment. Finally he clenched his fist. "It's not my fault. I'm programmed to do what is ordered of me."

"Bastien made you a machine. I know, and it's a shame. I wished I could have saved you, Walrum. I wished I had grabbed your body when I did and didn't leave you to suffer. I'm sorry I didn't. If it weren't for me, you wouldn't have ended up like this."

His eyes were turning red. Perhaps he could cry as well, but they wouldn't have been fake tears. I really was tearing him apart. I forcibly held back a sob.

"Stop doing this!" he shouted. "Stop telling me things I have no control over! I can't take it any longer!"

I reached out for him, but he had turned on his heel and stormed away. I stood there, silent, as the door slid shut. I held my hand over my mouth.

What was I doing? Was all this worth it?

Bastien came to get me when it was time to head to the event. I didn't leave him waiting, as I had gotten ready way before I needed to be. It gave me something to do and keep my mind off Walrum.

My heart ached for him. It wasn't his fault all this was happening—it wasn't his fault that Bastien was a sadistic bastard. He would pay for what he'd done to me and Walrum. I would make him suffer for all the pain he had put everyone through.

And if all went according to plan, it would be

soon.

I wasn't too worried about Nik—he had Jonathan on his side and the two of them could take Walrum. I knew they wouldn't kill him but try to take him in and save him. I doubted they would split up as they needed numbers to get through the building, and there was no one they could really trust except each other. They would extract us, then come back with another plan to capture Bastien. I was sure of it.

Bastien led me to a car that was waiting for us. He opened the door for me like he was some kind of gentleman. I got in, trying my best not to roll my eyes. The driver took us toward the event.

We, of course, would be entering from the back. We couldn't let the press see who we were. The press here never made sense to me, as in the Regit Republic and Nreff Nation always had people sneak in the back to get as much info as they could. In the YamaXie territory, however, that wasn't possible. Something always happened to those who didn't follow the rules. Each nation had their little secrets and tidbits, and that was this nation's. What was meant to be reported would be reported, and everything else just disappeared.

"Are you ready, *meine Puppen*?"

"Sure. You know how I always love events like these."

He patted my leg. "I hope I don't have to remind you to behave in front of the others."

I gave him a smile. "Don't worry. I'll be good. We just aren't in front of anyone yet. I just have to get out all my angst now."

"You know I love that sarcasm of yours."

"That's a lie and you know it."

"Of course, we both love to lie to each other. That's our little game, isn't it?"

I turned to peer out at the street. "Sure. That's our game."

CHAPTER XXIV

Nik

It was time.

The event would start soon, and Samuel and I would infiltrate the building that Mary and Rebecca were being held in. I took in a deep breath and let it out slowly.

It would be fine. Everything would be fine.

"According to the schematics, there is a security

room on each floor. If we can get to one of them, I should be able to access the cameras for the rest and put the video on a loop so you can get through without being detected."

I nodded. "Right. Any idea which one we should go to?"

"Well, the main floor would be the hardest, and I presume Admiral Wilde would stay anywhere near the main floor, so I would say floor two through five would be the easiest."

"Sounds good. It won't be hard to get to the second floor. Let's go."

We headed inside the building. I expected this place to be similar to a hotel, but I found as they stopped us, that was wrong.

"You need an ID to come in here," a man said as we tried to step inside.

"Sorry," I said. "I entered the wrong building. Our hotel is the next one over."

We turned and walked out of the building.

"Well, that is interesting," I commented.

"So it's not just some hotel. Someone important must own it."

I nodded. "Which means it will be a little more difficult getting in. Have any ideas?"

"Check around back and see if there is a staff entrance."

"Let's go."

We went around the building and entered the alleyway the staff used. Lucky for us, there was only one person getting ready for their day. I glanced around for cameras. There were two, and if I played my cards right, I would be able to snag him while he was behind his car where no one could see.

"Wait here," I whispered to Samuel.

He stayed where he was while I snuck around the car. As the man came around it, I shot him with the trank. Samuel caught him before he hit the ground and searched his pockets for keys. Eventually I found some for the car and the key card to get into the building. I placed his body in the car and straightened my shirt, acting as if I belonged there.

I nodded to Samuel to follow along. We walked with confidence over to the door and placed the key card on the scanner. It beeped and the door opened.

The first room that we entered was full of lockers. I presumed it had everyone's uniforms and where they could store their belongings. I rummaged around and found us two uniforms to change into. Luckily I was able to find ones that fit us.

The two of us headed toward an elevator, careful not to arouse suspicion. If one walked with confidence, no one typically noticed you were out of place, but if you snuck around, then they noticed right away.

We made it to the elevator and went to the third floor. As the elevator shut, I turned to Samuel. "Are you sure there isn't nothing on the third level?"

"The information I have says it's just bedrooms and storage closets."

"Well, we have uniforms on, so we hopefully won't stand out. Then once you take over the cameras, figure out where Rebecca is, then you can get me in."

He nodded. "That's the plan."

The elevator doors opened, and there was no one in the hallway. We walked down as Samuel glanced at his tablet. He turned and nodded to a door.

"This is the one. Still have the key card?"

I nodded and pulled it out. I tapped the pad, and luckily, it opened.

There were two men in the room, and as they saw us, they got up. I began to reach for my gun with the tranks when they spoke.

"About time you two showed up. Our shift has been over for fifteen minutes."

Samuel and I glanced at each other. We had lucked out in knocking on the person's door whose shift was in here.

"Yeah," I said. "Sorry about that. Had some car trouble."

He grunted as both of them left us. I wasn't sure if there was going to be another person who was going to come in here, so I quickly slid the door shut.

"Well, that was easy," Samuel said as he set his tablet down and began typing on the keyboard. I stood behind him and watched as if I knew all that he was doing.

A few moments passed, and I knew better than to

ask him if he was done yet, but I really wanted to. Instead, I took slow, deep breaths and tried to calm myself down for what was going to happen next.

I needed to save two people against who knew how many guards. No big deal.

"All right, they are on the fifty-first and fifty-third floor. Mary is on the lower one, and Rebecca is on the higher. Each floor has one guard outside their door but a few guards in different rooms as well. If you are careful, you won't alert them. They seem to just be back up, but since I'll have written over the cameras, they won't be alerted hopefully."

I nodded. The odds weren't too bad then.

"You have a trank gun, correct?"

He nodded. "Yup. I should be good. I'm overriding the cameras… now. You are safe to do what you need to do."

"Right. Well, good luck. Keep me informed on the ear comm."

"Will do."

I turned and headed toward the fifty-third floor, as I figured going after Rebecca would be the best. That way there would be two of us to keep Mary safe. There was no one in the elevator as I went up. It seemed there weren't too many people in this building—they must have mostly been at the event.

The door opened, and as Samuel had said, there was only one guard. I pulled out my gun with the tranks and shot him. The tranks didn't make a sound, so no one was alerted.

I searched the guard for a key card and eventually found it. I tapped it on the scanner and the door opened.

But to my surprise, it wasn't Rebecca who was standing in the room, but Walrum.

CHAPTER XXV

Rebecca

I didn't know what to do with my face.

I didn't want to smile, but I also didn't want to have a resting bitch face and make Bastien frustrated with me. On the other hand, I didn't want to have a fake smile and have people stare at me.

The fake smile was probably the best. I knew how to lie—it was practically the same thing.

Although I could talk my way out of a lot of things, I had never been that great at making sure my emotions didn't show on my face. I had to really concentrate and couldn't do it as a passive thing. It had gotten me into a lot of trouble, but I always made it out alive.

Just like I would tonight. Then, after Jonathan and Nik got Mary out of the building, I would be able to take my revenge on Bastien.

I tried to focus on that thought as it made me smile a true smile. I wanted more than anything for this night to end. Then it would all truly be over. Nik would make it out alive—I knew he would.

I had placed enough doubt and curiosity into Walrum's mind that he might help Nik or at least start talking to him to see if he can remember or something. That hesitation would be enough for Nik and Jonathan to knock him out.

I just prayed that they wouldn't kill him.

But he was a monster. He was Bastien's creation and had caused a lot of problems at the trial. I couldn't blame them if they wanted to take him out right then and there. I just wished Alexandra could have saved him before it was too late.

The trial felt as if it were months ago, but it was only a couple of weeks ago. Time always seemed to go by slower when Bastien was involved.

We stepped inside the banquet hall, and I stared in wonder. If only I were here under other pretenses, as it was quite beautiful and I probably would have had a good time with anyone else, even Jonathan. Chandeliers hovered from the ceiling, and bright gold and red decorations filled the walls. Even the tables with food were covered with similar decorations. A golden dragon statue stood at the center of it all.

"It's quite fantastic, isn't it? I always did love coming to these banquets with you. The past few years have been lonely without you."

I held back a gag and kept my smile. "I'm sorry to disappoint."

He patted my arm as he interlinked it with his. "I know you lie, but that's all right. You are here now."

Not by my own will. I wanted to say that but knew better. As we walked, I noted how many of the people at the dinner were here and how many politicians were here.

"I am surprised they would want you here. You are a wanted man."

"This is for YamaXie officials only, and I'm one of their guests. No one from the Nreff Nation will be here, and as we know, no one with the media is allowed to enter. We will be safe here, don't you worry."

Yeah, I felt so safe. I glanced around, seeing if I could spot any food that would be vegan. There were a few items.

"Are you hungry already? Let's go see what there is to eat."

At least there was some good out of tonight, as I did like a nice buffet. We headed over and grabbed a plate as someone approached us.

"Admiral Wilde, I see that you made it. It's great to see someone as prestigious as you at an event like this."

Wilde turned to the guest. I stood there with my plate, wondering if I could get food or if I needed to wait. My stomach grumbled, and I decided I didn't need to be a part of this conversation. I stepped back and turned to the buffet.

I grabbed some tofu fried rice, spring rolls, sautéed spinach in garlic sauce, and a couple of other things that I knew would be vegan, but I wasn't sure what they were called. As I finished filling my plate, I felt an arm go around my waist.

"Well, someone couldn't wait, could they?" Bastien commented as he held his empty plate.

"I figured I would get a head start. You don't need me messing up talking to anyone, now do you?"

He laughed. "That's quite true. But I rather not you leave my sight."

"I didn't leave your sight. I made sure of that."

"Well, I'm glad you have some self-restraint. I hope you'll keep it for the rest of the night."

"Don't worry, I will."

I followed him to a table where we could sit and eat. A few people joined us, and Bastien made small talk. I wasn't great at small talk—in fact, it was the thing I hated to do the most. I let my eyes wander around the room, and that was when I saw them.

Coughing, I had almost choked on a piece of tofu. I cleared it and shook my head. Jonathan and Bardon were here disguised as waiters. Were they really that stupid? I couldn't believe they would do that.

Did that mean Nik was here, or was he by himself, getting Mary? And if that was the case, then he and Walrum would be facing off by themselves. I debated what I should do. Bastien made it clear that I wasn't supposed to leave his sight.

He patted my back. "Are you all right? You nearly choked on your food."

I nodded. "I'm fine—I just need a moment. May I go to the restroom?"

He watched me for a moment. "Fine, by all means. Just hurry back, all right?"

I got up and headed to the bathroom. As I walked toward the hallway where I had spotted the bathrooms earlier, I stared at Bardon and Jonathan, hoping they would make eye contact with me. Jonathan did, and I saw him nod.

So they understood they needed to follow me, but while Bastien wasn't looking at me. I let out a breath as I went inside the ladies' room, hoping no one was there. I searched all the stalls and found it was clear. A couple of moments later, Jonathan appeared.

"What are you doing here?" Jonathan asked.

I shook my head. "What am I doing here? You mean what are you doing here? Where's Nik?"

"He's… saving you in your hotel room."

"Ach du liebe." I put my hands on my hips. "Well, it was a trap, and I figured he would be okay because you wouldn't be dumb enough to try to stop Bastien here."

"Well, surprise. I'm dumb enough."

"Clearly."

"Well, I think he'll be fine, for what it's worth. He's determined to find you."

I went to the mirror and checked my makeup. "And what about you? How are you going to kidnap Bastien with all those people around?"

"We have a plan. I'm not going to tell you. No offense, Rebecca. I may trust you, but I don't trust

Bastien."

"That's fair." I turned to him. "You do realize he'll use me as a shield, right? And if he does, please just shoot both of us."

He shook his head. "I can't—"

"I'm serious, Jonathan. Take the shot."

I held his gaze. He finally nodded. "All right. I will."

"Good. Well, he is waiting for me, so I better get back out there. Wait a bit before you leave, just in case." I patted his back. "I'm looking forward to the show. Impress me, will you?"

With that, I left him standing there in the women's bathroom. Bastien was watching me as I made my way back to the table. He put his arm around my shoulders.

"Feeling better?"

I nodded. "*Ja*. A lot better."

CHAPTER XXVI

Nik

"What are you doing here? Where's Rebecca?" I asked as the door slid shut behind me.

Walrum didn't appear the same as I had last seen him. The last time I had seen him, hatred and anger filled his eyes, fueled by whatever orders Sebastien had given him. Now he appeared to be distraught—almost confused and not knowing what he needed to do.

"Rebecca is with Bastien."

I reached toward my gun.

Walrum was quick to raise his own gun. "Don't think about it."

Well, I fucked up. I let out a breath. "So, are you here to kill me?"

"That's the orders I was given."

I realized how he phrased that. "You make it sound like you don't want to."

He frowned. "I just… I don't know anymore, all right!"

Wow. Where did that come from? I had a feeling Rebecca did something, and it would come in handy.

"Do you remember your past?" I asked, not moving—not giving him a reason to shoot.

He shook his head. "I don't. I know it all—I was given all the information I needed, but it's like reading a story that has nothing to do with you. I don't get it."

"What don't you get?"

"I don't understand why I'm like this! What

happened for me to forget everything? Why was this done to me?"

Whoa, Rebecca really did a number on him. "Look, I don't have all the answers to that, but if you come with me, I can take you back—"

"*Nein*!" He moved the gun up higher toward my head. I froze. "You all did your poking and prodding and found nothing. What am I supposed to do now?"

He definitely had a point there. "But that was when we thought you were getting better because you were trying to trick us. Now we know what to look for. We can help you."

His eyes were red. "No one can help me! Not you! Not Rebecca! I don't know who I am anymore!"

"Then let me help you! You were my best friend, and I'll do anything to help you get back to be who you were and help you take Sebastien down. But first you need to trust me. Can you do that?"

I heard a crackle in my earbuds. "Nik, there are fifteen guards coming your way. They have their guns out and are ready to fire."

Shit. "Get down!" I yelled at Walrum as I tackled him to the ground. As we hit the ground, bullets came through the door and walls.

This had been a double setup—Sebastien was trying to take down Walrum as well. He must have known something was up. That bastard.

The bullets finally stopped, and the two of us rushed behind the couch.

Walrum turned to me. "You saved me."

I let out a breath as I checked my gun to make sure it was loaded. "Yup, that's what friends do. Now, do you have my back?"

He nodded as he raised his gun. "Yes. Then you promise to help me?"

"Of course. Now, let's take these guys out."

I tapped the ear comm. "Are they lined up, or are they surrounding the door now?"

"A little of both."

"Turn on the sprinklers on this floor. Can you do that?"

Before I finished my sentence, the sprinklers began raining down water upon us. I smiled as I motioned to Walrum to follow me.

I kicked down the door and began shooting, as did Walrum. We shot down ten of them before they realized what had happened and began shooting at us. I turned and hid behind the doorframe, waiting for our chance.

There was a pause as they had to reload their guns. I aimed for the last five and took them down. The water stopped.

I pressed the ear comm. "Great job, Samuel. Now we wil head to Mary's cell."

Walrum answered before Samuel could. "I'll take her to you. But do me a favor and act as if you are my prisoner. It might go over a bit better."

We headed toward the elevator. "Except that they think you should be dead too."

He shrugged. "Fair enough. Then I guess we'll take them all out."

"Should we be trusting this guy?" I heard Samuel ask. "I mean, he did break out of the military base and is brainwashed."

"We will be fine. Trust me," I answered him. "How many guards are on Mary's floor?"

"Just two. They all had headed up to you."

"Perfect."

Walrum and I went down a few levels, and as the elevator door opened, I saw the two guards standing in front of the doorway. Walrum and I each shot one.

"This brings back a lot of memories," I commented.

"Wish I could say the same."

We got to Mary's room, and Walrum unlocked it. Mary was hiding in the corner.

"Nik!" she said as she ran to me. "I heard gunshots and feared for the worst."

"It was me. Now let's get you out of here."

She turned and noticed Walrum. "What about him?"

"He's with us now. Don't worry about it."

"Okay… Where are my *fratello* and Samuel."

I took out the ear comm and gave it to her. She placed it in her ear.

"Samuel?" Her eyes began to water as she heard her love's voice. It made me smile. I turned to the door.

"Now come on—we have to get out of here

before more guards come."

CHAPTER XXVII

Rebecca

Now, did I make a scene, or did I wait for whatever Jonathan and Bardon had in store?

Choices, choices. I knew Bardon would be incredibly mad at me if I blew it, but they didn't count on being here, so whatever they were going to do already had backfired. If I knew Bardon, he was going to try to take Bastien in, which would be easy with this crowd. They liked him there—they liked him everywhere. Or at least, they feared him everywhere.

Bastien was going to use me as a shield—I just knew it. He knew Bardon wouldn't hurt me, and he wouldn't give Jonathan the orders to hurt me either. Which meant I would have to live with the fact that I would be the reason Bastien got away. Again.

And I didn't know if Mary was safe.

That was the important part. But if Nik was going there, he would more than likely save her, so I didn't have too much to worry about. I could take my chances, but if I was wrong, would I be able to live with myself?

But at the same time, there was a dinner knife in front of me. I could use it—I could stab him through the heart right now, and it would all be over. I would be arrested, yes, but I was going to prison either way. Which prison would be better? Well, both would suck.

Bastien placed his hand on mine. "You seem deep in thought, *meine Liebchen.* Is something wrong?"

"No, just tired." Of your shit.

"You sure are staring at that knife intently. You are thinking about stabbing me with it, aren't you?"

"Never. I know stabbing you would do me no good. Unless I stabbed you in the heart, but we both know you don't have one."

He squeezed my hand a little harder. "You are just so funny, aren't you?"

"You know me—I could have been a comedian if I wasn't in the military. Maybe that's what I should do after I retire."

"You think you'll ever retire from this? Do you really think you'll ever be able to settle down? Maybe you are a comedian."

He had a point there. I turned to glance around.

Bastien leaned in and whispered to me "When were you going to tell me Admiral Bardon and Jonathan were here?"

My heart felt as if it had stopped. "Are they? I thought you already knew they would be?"

"I did. But I expect you to say something once you spotted them."

"Who says I have?"

"What did Jonathan tell you in the bathroom?"

I shook my head. "There was no one in the bathroom, so nothing?"

He squeezed my hand tighter. It felt as if it were going to break. "Tell me now, Rebecca. I'm not playing around."

"Just that Nik was back at the hotel, trying to save me."

Bastien let go of my hand. "Well, at least it is all going according to plan. Now, should we make our distraction or wait for theirs?"

"What do you mean?" I asked.

He laughed. "You'll see, *meine Liebchen*. Just give it a little bit."

That wasn't good. He knew they were coming—he knew their plan, but how? I assumed Bardon didn't tell anyone anything—so how could Bastien know so much? Was he that good at predicting what other people would do?

It was probably the latter—his hobby was human observation after all. I had seen him predict many things. He knew how to read people, which was impressive since he didn't have any empathy.

"Let's wait," he finally said. "I'm curious what they have in store for us."

I took in a deep breath and let it out slowly. He leaned in to whisper in my ear again. "Don't worry. I'll keep you safe." He backed away. "Now come, let's go get some dessert."

I got up and followed him. There was no point in saying no.

There were a few things I could eat, including some mochi. I grabbed a couple and followed Bastien as he went to talk with some officials.

Why couldn't Jonathan and Bardon hurry it up? I wanted this to be over with. I presumed they wouldn't wait too long so it would lessen their chances of being spotted. Or perhaps they were waiting for the okay to go from Nik.

As if hearing my thoughts, suddenly there was a loud bang like a bomb had gone off and smoke filled the banquet room. I grabbed the closest cloth I could find during the panic. And a knife. I quickly turned and swung it straight at Bastien, but he blocked it with his arm. I might not have gotten him in the chest like I wanted, but I did make him bleed at least a little.

"You little *Miststück*," he growled as he grabbed me. "Now where do you think they might be?"

Bastien kept me close—using me as a shield as he walked toward the back exit. People were screaming and running, but Bastien was patient. He knew to keep his eyes out for the real threat.

I noticed there was no actual damage anywhere in here, and it all had been a diversion to get people to run away. As most of the people cleared away and Bastien was still slow to make sure he didn't fall into some trap, I heard Bardon's voice.

"Freeze, Admiral Sebastien Wilde! You are under arrest!"

Bastien turned us to face Bardon and Jonathan. He laughed. "Do you really think the two of you can stop me?" He pulled me even closer. "Or, I suppose, do you think you can do it without shooting Rebecca here?"

"Please, for the love of God, just shoot me!" I yelled at them.

Bardon and Jonathan didn't do that but still kept their guns up.

Bardon replied, "Let her go, and this won't have to get to get messy."

Bastien said, "Oh, but it already has."

CHAPTER XXVIII

Nik

We made it back to where Samuel was and were able to leave the building without any more trouble. Once we were outside, we heard the alarms and saw the smoke coming out of the building the event was at.

Jonathan and Bardon had started their part of the *plan*.

"Come on," I said. "Let's go meet up with the others like we *planned*."

Walrum grabbed my arm. "Wait. He knows you are coming."

I turned to him and shook my head. "Impossible. There's no way. That information could have gotten leaked."

"It didn't—he's just clever and knows how you all plan. But I knew what his own plan is. He's going to make a diversion and run for his ship to set out somewhere else."

I couldn't believe what I was hearing. Walrum was telling us the rest of his plan—we were finally one step ahead of Sebastien.

I nodded. "Let's go then."

"Wait," Samuel called out. "You are supposed to stick to the plan."

"I'm not giving this chance up. If Jonathan and Bardon fail, this could be our only chance, and I'm taking it. Tell Bardon I'm sorry. Just get Mary to safety and hopefully all this will be over soon."

"Are you sure you can trust him?" Samuel added.

I turned to Walrum and nodded. "Yeah. I think I

can."

Walrum smiled a little as we started running toward the shuttle to the spaceport. I didn't know what to expect—I didn't know how we were going to do it—but we were going to stop Sebastien once and for all.

We made it to the shuttle, and I watched as the spaceport came closer and closer. "How long do you think we are ahead of him?"

"Probably not too long. There are some private shuttles to take up here, and he'll take one of those. There's a crew waiting for him, so we'll have to convince them we're supposed to be there."

I nodded. "Right. Hopefully they didn't know about the plan where you were supposed to die with me. Then I can just be your prisoner."

"That's what I'm thinking. Then once we are in and the ship is going, we can ambush him. We'll just have to make it so the rest of the crew is locked out of where we will take him out."

"That can be arranged. He'll come through the cargo bay, and the rest of the crew will be at their stations at the ready. I presume the moment the cargo bay closes, they'll set off."

I watched as the spaceport came even closer. "So just lock the doors and be at the ready."

"Sounds like a plan to me."

CHAPTER XXIX

Rebecca

There was another explosion.

By the looks on Bardon's and Jonathan's faces, it wasn't them. Bastien had also set up bombs, but by the rumbling, I had a feeling they were real and not just an illusion.

Bardon turned his attention back to Bastien. "Sebastien! Stop this now! You will not be able to keep fleeing forever."

"Oh, but I think I'll be able to. That is, unless you want to shoot Rebecca to get to me."

"Just do it!" I shouted. "One of you just shoot me!"

Bastien laughed. "They won't—Bardon is too much of a softie. Speaking of which…" He nodded behind the two of them. "That little mechanic of yours seems to need some assistance."

I saw a guard drag Russ out from behind a pillar. I whispered, "What the hell is he doing here?"

He must have snuck onto whatever ship Jonathan and Bardon came on, as it was his sister who had been captured. It made sense.

Bardon and Jonathan turned their attention to Russ. As they were distracted, Bastien spun around and dragged me out of the building. I didn't scream for Bardon or Jonathan, knowing that Russ should be their priority at that moment. As we left, I heard a gunshot and prayed that Russ was all right.

Bastien rammed his gun into my side as he moved me forward down the street. I thought about fighting him right then and there but didn't need the local authorities who were starting to surround the building to take me in. That would be an even worse mess.

No, I would wait until we were alone. Mary was no longer a threat, and I could finally get my revenge.

Bastien forced me to the shuttle that would take us to the spaceport. I furrowed my brows.

"We aren't we going back to the hotel?"

"No, *meine Liebchen*, we are getting out of here."

I let out a laugh. "What, have your plans been foiled?"

"On the contrary—I knew this would happen and planned it all already. We have a private shuttle waiting, and my ship is ready to go."

This day was getting worse and worse. He led me toward the private ship, and it took us up toward the spaceport. I still couldn't do anything, as I didn't want to risk the pilot on this shuttle. But once we got to our ship, I could take him out. I wouldn't care if anyone was on the ship, which I knew there would be. If they stopped me, then I would pay the price. If they didn't, well, once Bastien was dead, they wouldn't have to follow his orders any longer.

We made it to the spaceport, and Sebastien led me to his ship. I tried not to smile as I knew I would have my revenge at last, and I didn't care what it cost me. As we entered the ship, the cargo doors quickly closed, and I felt the ship begin to stir. He was wasting no time.

"Well, *meine Liebchen*, we seem to have made it. Your knights in shining armor didn't succeed yet again."

I elbowed him straight in the gut, but he didn't drop his gun. I tried to grab for it, but his grip was tight. He swung his arm and smacked me. I lost my balance in the struggle as I was still wearing the damn heels. He pointed the gun down at me.

"Do I need to teach you another lesson, you hypocritical bitch?"

I glared at him, daring him to do it, because I would just get back up and try it again. Before either of us could make our move, a voice came out from behind some equipment.

"Stop right there, Admiral Wilde. You're outnumbered." It was Nik. My eyes widened. He was alive and here. I couldn't believe it.

Sebastien laughed. "You survived my trap! Well done. I commend you. Was that because Rebecca started putting doubt in my experiment?"

As he said that, Walrum stepped out as well. "I'm going to get back what you took away from me—mark my words."

"Oh really? Well, this should be interesting. I guess you've left me no choice." Bastien licked his lips. *"Zerstören."*

Walrum let out a scream as he held his head. This was not good.

CHAPTER XXX

Nik

Well, this wasn't going to end well.

I didn't know if I should keep my gun on Sebastien or if I should move it to Walrum. Whatever Sebastien did set something off in Walrum's mind. Question was, did it destroy him or did it make him want to destroy everything around him?

That answer was revealed quickly.

Walrum turned the gun toward me. I dove out of the way as bullets rained down upon me. Sebastien joined him in shooting at me. Rebecca didn't hesitate as she talked to Sebastien and tried to get the gun out of his hands.

"Get off of me, you stupid bitch!" He smacked her, but she didn't stop.

I turned to my own threat, wondering what I should do. I could shoot him, but I had promised I would help fix him. There had to be a way to get him out of here without ending his life. I jumped behind a large box full of cargo and pulled out my trank gun. I turned to point it at Walrum, but he had already caught up to me and kicked the gun out of my hand.

Before he could fire off his own gun, I tackled him. It was clear he still remembered his military training, or at least his body did. Problem was, he was always a little better than I was.

I tried not to think about it—tried to not worry about the fact he could easily overpower me if he remembered my weaknesses. Although I had trained a bit here and there, I definitely hadn't been keeping up with everything, and I had a feeling Sebastien made him train quite often.

Before I could figure a way to incapacitate him, Walrum had me in a headlock and was moving his gun to my head.

Was this the end? Was I done for? After everything that had happened.

I heard a thunk, and Walrum's grip loosened enough where I could flip him over and get him to drop his gun. I glanced around and found it had been Rebecca—she had thrown her shoe at Walrum.

But it had caused Rebecca her own fight, as I watched Sebastien kick her in the stomach and shoot her straight in the leg.

"No!" I screamed as I watched blood seep out of her leg.

"There! That should keep you out of my hair for a moment." He turned to me, which was not a good sign.

I quickly pointed Walrum's gun at him but not before I felt something heavy smack me in the head. Everything went dark.

CHAPTER XXXI

Rebecca

Walrum had just knocked out Nik, and Sebastien was aiming for him. Was this it? Was I going to lose everything I had ever wanted in my life?

I didn't care about the pain—I was fueled by pure adrenaline—and stood up and tackled Bastien. I clawed and scratched and tore the gun away from him. I punched and smacked, screaming at him.

"You fucking asshole! I won't let you hurt him! You will not take another love away from me."

He smacked me hard, and I flew off him. Bastien reached for the gun, but I didn't let him have the time. I tackled him again, screaming still.

"Walrum, finish the job!" he ordered. "Kill Nik!"

I didn't know what to do. If I left Bastien, I knew he would grab the gun and shoot Nik, but Walrum was staring down at Nik's unconscious body.

But he wasn't moving—he was thinking. He was getting his clearer thoughts back.

I had bet Nik's life on Walrum fighting the orders inside him and held down Bastien as best as I could.

"Help me, Walrum! Please!"

"You little bitch, you really got to him. Well, that is no matter. I have other orders for him."

Before he could say them, I covered his mouth and shouted at Walrum. "Please! Help me! Grab the gun!"

Walrum hesitated and grabbed his head. "Stop it! Make it stop!"

"Grab the gun! Please!"

Bastien bit my hand but not before Walrum went to grab the gun. I watched Bastien's eyes widen as Walrum pointed the gun at him.

And with a loud bang, he was gone.

I stared at Bastien's body, unmoving and lifeless. It was over. All of it was over. I laughed and cried at the same time.

It was finished. It was really finished.

I got up and limped to Walrum. I wrapped my arms around him. "We did it. We did it."

He stepped back and moved the gun to Nik. My eyes widened.

"What are you doing?"

"I can't shake off the last orders. I have to—" Before he could answer, he moved the gun to his own head and shot himself in the head.

I screamed.

CHAPTER XXXII

Nik

The first thing I heard was Rebecca screaming.

My eyes flickered open, and I grabbed my head as it was pounding. Walrum had hit me, that much I could remember.

As my sight adjusted, I found Sebastien's body on the ground. He was dead. They had done it.

What I didn't expect to find was Rebecca crying

over Walrum's body. I hurried over to her. Had Sebastien killed him before she killed Sebastien? What exactly happened?

As I approached, it was clear the wound was not from Sebastien. Walrum and shot himself in the head. I wrapped my arms around Rebecca.

"It's okay. It's over. We did it."

"He didn't have to do this! We could have helped him!"

"I know… I know…"

The doors to the cargo bay opened, and I was quick to point my gun at them. "Don't move! We killed Sebastien Wilde—you no longer have to follow his orders. I'm Captain Nikolas Ritter of Nreff Nation. Get us turned back around to the spaceport, and we might not arrest you."

The men looked at the body, then quickly nodded. "Yes, sir."

The men hurried off, and I turned back to Rebecca. Tears kept falling from her eyes as she stared down at her once fiancé, but she had stopped screaming. I squeezed her tight.

"Rebecca, whatever you need, just let me know."

"I just need a moment, all right?"

I nodded and let her be as I felt the ship begin to turn back. I let out a breath. This was finally over, but they had lost Walrum—right when he thought perhaps we could save him.

Life wasn't fair.

We got back to the spaceport, and Bardon and Jonathan were there waiting for us. My heart pounded in my chest.

He wasn't going to actually do it, was he? He wasn't going to actually arrest Rebecca, right?

He barked orders to extract the two bodies that were in the cargo bay. Rebecca didn't say anything as she stepped up to Bardon and lifted her wrists.

"We finally did it. I guess I'm your only witness now, right?" she said.

He watched her with pity in his eyes. "No—I think you've had enough trauma for a lifetime. Get out of here. I'll say your body was lost in transit but that you had been killed as well."

Both our eyes widened.

"What?" she asked.

"Run and don't return to the Nreff Nation. Or if you do, don't let me know." Bardon turned to me. "And you—make sure to keep her safe. You are dismissed from the military."

"See," Jonathan commented. "You should have just stuck it out. But you tried to do your own thing."

I laughed as I grabbed Rebecca's hand. We were finally together at last.

CHAPTER XXXIII

Rebecca

Nik and I were able to go to the hospital without any trouble. The doctors helped get the morphine-B out of my system, thank goodness, and Nik got his head wound treated. Samuel was able to make us some IDs before he, Mary, and Russ, whom I was glad was fine, left the YamaXie system and went back home. I would miss them, but knew it was best to cut ties with all of them to keep them safe.

Although it seemed Samuel could easily hack into any system and find us if he wanted, I was impressed with what Nik told me about him and wished he had been on a lot of missions with us.

But instead of doing what we normally did while on the run before, Nik and I found a place in the Regit Republic on the coast where we knew we would never be bothered. I sat in my beach chair under the umbrella, staring out at the ocean.

I couldn't believe he was gone—Walrum killed himself to save Nik. Perhaps he was starting to remember. Perhaps if we had been able to save him, life would have gone back to normal.

"Hey beautiful," Nik said as he brought us margaritas.

I took mine from his hands. "Hey. Thanks for grabbing those. Hanging on the beach is less fine without margaritas."

"I highly agree."

He took a seat next to me and grabbed my hand and squeezed it. I smiled at him.

Perhaps this was how it was always meant to be

—just the two of us finally together.

Thank You For Reading!

Thank you so much for reading! Readers like you make it possible for authors like me to write stories! If you could spare a moment and leave a review on Amazon, Goodreads, BookBub, and wherever you like to buy books, that would mean the world to me! It really helps authors like me to succeed in the publishing world.

Acknowledgements

I want to thank everyone who helped me with this novel! This series all started at ASU's Your Novel Year Program back in 2015. I want to say thank you to my mentors Mike, Joe, Chantelle, Kevin, and Paul who helped me with all my writing questions and taught me how to write. Thank you to everyone in the program who gave me feed back (dad, Cassie, Gil, Gina, Jeff, Laura, Marcel, Stacy, Deborah, Paul, Jasmine, and Tom), and to my writing group who also helped with this project (Traci, Rebecca, Bernie, and Christi). Thank you to my editor Anne Victory and cover artist Biserka Designs who made this book possible. Thank you to Kaleb who answered all my random questions. I swear it was for a book! Another thank you to my friends Earlene, Shayne, Faye, Veronica, Tom, Carl, Ruben, Justin, and all the others who have helped with this book over the years. Lastly, thank you to my parents who have always supported me, and to my husband who gets the privilege of reading all my books :).

<u>About the Author</u>

Lyra Thorsson is the sci-fi pen name for Dani Hoots. She is a science fiction, fantasy, romance, and young adult author who loves anything with a story. She has a B.S. in Anthropology, a Masters of Urban and Environmental Planning, a Certificate in Novel Writing from Arizona State University, and a BS in Herbal Science from Bastyr University.

Her hobbies include reading, watching anime, cooking, studying different languages, wire walking, hula hoop, and working with plants. She is also an herbalist and sells her concoctions on FoxCraft Apothecary. She lives in Phoenix with her husband and visits Seattle often.

Feel free to email her with any questions you might have!
danihootsauthor@gmail.com